Hannibal's Rat

Geoffrey Guy

Hodder
Children's
Books

A division of Hodder Headline Limited

Part I

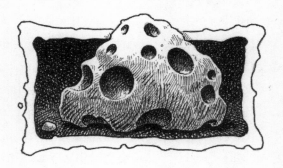

1

'New People,' said Scratchbelly bitterly. 'I hate New People.'

His mate Slickwhiskers elegantly arranged her tail. 'No cat, though,' she said. 'The last lot had a cat. And these new ones are very neat and tidy.'

'Old Lightning was harmless,' said Scratchbelly. 'He was so fat, by the time he made his move I was half a room away. And clean! Who wants clean? I used to have breakfast off the carpet without having to go two jumps from the hole. But this lot have that Noisy Sucker going all hours of the day. You're lucky if you can find any grub anywhere – even under the fridge. Don't talk to me about clean.'

'It will be all right.' Old Grey, a mouse of venerable age, spoke slowly and portentously. 'We shall adapt. We shall learn their ways.'

This was clearly a Wise Saying and should have been afforded a respectful silence; but it didn't get one, for there was a clatter of feet at the entrance hole and a young mouse appeared suddenly in the chamber. He was evidently in panic and distress.

'Dad!' he cried. 'I'm sorry Dad! I've been Spotted!'

His parents groaned in unison. To be Spotted was a disgrace and a disaster. Scratchbelly advanced wrathfully on his offspring.

'You fool, Number Three! You realize what this means? Poison, traps, blocked-up holes – they might even get a cat in!'

'I couldn't help it, Dad. It was the Noisy

Sucker. It started suddenly, and I didn't hear the Female coming up behind me.'

'What did the Female do?'

'It squeaked very loudly and climbed on a chair.'

'They always do that,' said Old Grey wisely. 'I think it's so that they can jump on you harder.'

'Such a pity he was Spotted, though,' said Slickwhiskers. 'Just at Great Feast time.

They've just put up the Sparkly Stuff and the Uneatable Tree.'

Scratchbelly thought hard. 'Call the rest of the kids here,' he said at last. 'We must make the best of it: get out there and forage before they start exterminating us. Get some stores in while there's time.'

A few moments later the family emerged cautiously from the entrance hole, led uneasily by Number Three as decreed by Scratchbelly on the grounds that he who had been Spotted should take the greatest risk. All seemed quiet. The mice rose as one on to their haunches, their heads turning in the same direction. Delicious smells were flowing into their nostrils: the source was clearly the table in the centre of the room.

'Go on, Number Three,' said Scratchbelly. In a trice his son had crossed the carpet, climbed the leg and was looking down from the table top.

'It's good, Dad! It's great! Cheese – nuts – raisins – it's marvellous!'

'Up we go,' said Scratchbelly. He, Old Grey,

Slickwhiskers and his four remaining offspring were soon on the table. It was as Number Three said: the food was there in a neat, irresistible pile.

'Wait!' said Old Grey sternly. 'Remember, we have been Spotted. There may be Poison.'

'Number Three,' said Scratchbelly.

They watched as the young mouse, pale-faced, crept to a piece of cheese and bit into it; watched and waited for the expected kicking and convulsing. Nothing happened. Number Three grinned proudly. 'It's all right! I'm all right! I'm fine!' He began eating at full speed.

The others joined him and for a while there was silence broken only by the sounds of nibbling and belching. Eventually Scratchbelly paused for breath.

'Well.' He rubbed his tummy contentedly as he spoke. 'Maybe the New People aren't so bad after all.'

'Maybe,' said Slickwhiskers. 'Don't eat those green leaves, children. They spike your nose.'

'The red berries are nice, though,' said Number Two. She was a greedy and impetuous youngster and her parents doubted if she would survive long enough to be given a name.

'Wonder what this paper's for?' said Slickwhiskers. 'Come in handy for nest-making,' she said softly to Scratchbelly.

A door in the next room gently creaked. In a flash the table was deserted. Only a scattering of scraps and a note were left behind.

The note said 'Happy Christmas, Mickey and Minnie!'

For the week of the Great Feast the Scratchbelly family prospered. The New People ate, and wasted, even more than their predecessors. Food was everywhere for the taking. Of sprout leaves there was, indeed, a surfeit; Scratchbelly was not alone in declaring that he could not face another sprout, and the mice's living quarters were more than usually malodorous.

A time of plenty indeed; yet Scratchbelly was

uneasy. The fact remained that Number Three had been seen by the humans. There was a deal of truth in the ancient and wise, if ungrammatical, mouse saying: 'Once Spotted, never Forgotted.'

Sure enough, his worries were justified as soon as the Feast period ended. First, the holes were blocked up. In itself this was more of an inconvenience than a disaster since the humans blocked only the holes inside the house, and then only the visible ones. It meant longer foraging journeys from outside holes with a certain amount of open-air travel and squeezing under doors. But hole-blocking was, as Old Grey repeated ad nauseam, only the beginning of the troubles.

Poison and Traps came together. It was a bad time for the Scratchbelly tribe. Poison was not *too* dangerous for an experienced mouse: the treated food was identifiable to the knowing eye by its unlikely siting and excessive amount. But for young mice it was different, especially a mouse as greedy and stupid as Number Two. She expired quickly after eating from a small pile of grains by the skirting board.

The loss of Number Two was sobering but not unexpected. Neither Scratchbelly nor his mate Slickwhiskers had expected her to last long. But the trapping of Scratchbelly's brother, Flashfoot – whose family lived in an adjacent wall to the Scratchbellys' – sent a shock wave through the community.

'It beats me,' said Scratchbelly. 'Surely he knew what a catting trap looks like.'

'It wasn't the normal sort,' said Number Three, who had as usual been where he shouldn't have. 'It wasn't a Slam and Stick-you. I saw it. Flashfoot went after this cheese and a sort of door fell down behind him. He couldn't get out. Then a human came so I had to hide. When I was able to come out again, Flashfoot had disappeared.'

'We'll all have to be very careful,' said Scratchbelly. 'But least they haven't got a cat.'

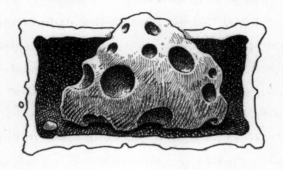

2

It was perhaps fortunate that Scratchbelly himself was the first to encounter the cat. The following day, he was in a reasonably safe spot a few feet away from an unblocked hole behind the cooker when the kitchen door opened quietly. Cat and mouse saw each other simultaneously.

The last people's cat had been a stout tabby who indulged in a lengthy crouching and stretching ritual before attacking. But this cat was different. It seemed to Scratchbelly that it was on him almost immediately, a lean black killing machine moving at tremendous speed. Scratchbelly sprang desperately for the hole, knowing in his heart that he was too late, he wouldn't make it.

Behind him there was a swishing sound and, to his surprise, he found himself in safety and unhurt. Something struck the wall outside the hole with a crash, and there was a torrent of angry and very indecent language in cat-speak.

Then silence. But, of course, the cat hadn't gone away. Scratchbelly knew this; the cat would wait and watch on the slim chance that another really stupid mouse might come out again. It was – except for very young cats – more of a ritual than anything. It did, however, provide a chance for peace talks between Prey and Predator. Scratchbelly decided to use the opportunity. He was a believer in talking to the enemy. Not all mice were of the same opinion; Old Grey said that Familiarity bred Contempt, and any mouse who held a cat in contempt wouldn't last long. But Scratchbelly believed that understanding your cat could save your life or at least make it more comfortable. For example, if the cat mentioned he kept away from draughts you would probably be fairly safe coming under a door.

'Trap my tail but you're fast,' he said. 'I thought you'd got me. You don't hang about, do you?'

'Well, I'm a farm cat,' said the cat. 'No time for all this crouch – stalk – spring nonsense. If you want to eat you've got to move fast, not give 'em time to think. And you're right, I would have got you if it hadn't been for that dogging loose rug. Lost me back feet, straight into the wall. How these dogging humans expect me to catch anything with dogging loose rugs all over the dogging place—'

'Calm down!' said Scratchbelly.

'Well anyway, but for that you were protein. Or rather' – the cat's voice took on a worried note – 'for display purposes. Thing is, I'm on probation. Got to give them some evidence or it's back to the farm.'

'And you don't want to leave?'

'Not likely.' The cat yawned luxuriously; Scratchbelly heard – imagined – the open mouth, and shuddered. 'Go back to draughty barns, dodging terriers and a rat-meat diet? No thanks.'

'So, if you don't catch any mice, you'll get taken back?'

'Don't even think it,' said the cat nastily. 'You're pretty fast but not fast enough to beat me. And there'll be others slower or stupider. I'll have a row of you on the fireplace before you know it.'

'You killed rats on the farm, then,' said Scratchbelly, more to change the subject than anything else.

'Sure. Rats are no problem so long as you're quick and bite hard,' said the cat complacently, cleaning an ear with one paw. 'What I could really do with right now is a nice big rat.'

'To eat?'

'To SHOW. I put a rat on the fireplace, I'll be a big hero. Be here for life. Kittymeat by the tinful, my own bed in front of the fire – I'd be a fat cat before you could look round. That's what I want,' said the cat dreamily. 'To be a fat cat. No chasing you lot, no need to catch food.'

'And one rat would do it?' said Scratchbelly thoughtfully.

'Sure,' said the cat again. He rose from his haunches in a single, sinister movement. 'Well, I must be off. Check if any of your lot are moving in the sitting-room. See you around – if you don't see me first.'

'What's your name?' Scratchbelly called after him.

'They've called me Hannibal,' said the cat sourly. 'Damn silly name. Doesn't mean anything. What's yours?'

'Scratchbelly.'

'Now that's something like a name,' said

Hannibal. 'Descriptive. Hannibal indeed! What was wrong with Blackie?'

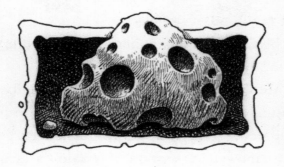

3

When Scratchbelly arrived at the main living-chamber, he found Old Grey there, instructing one of the youngsters.

'And remember, never carry more than you—' He broke off, seeing Scratchbelly's expression. 'What's up, son?'

'Trouble,' said Scratchbelly. 'Number One, gather the family here, quick. We need a meeting.'

Number One went off like a rocket, glad to

escape Old Grey's tutelage. In a very short time the family was assembled.

'I couldn't find Number Five,' said Number One. 'He must be foraging.'

'We'll start without him,' said Scratchbelly. 'Listen all of you. A cat has arrived and he's bad news. Very fast. So double-check your every move from now on. If you don't see him before he sees you, you've had it. That's the first thing. The second is this: there's a way of getting rid of him. I won't go into details, but we have to get a rat into the house for him to catch.' He turned to Old Grey. 'Are there any rats round here?'

Old Grey nodded slowly. 'At the bottom of the garden,' he said. 'At least, there used to be. But it's a bad journey. Lots of open ground. And rats are tricky devils, and nasty with it. You ever seen a rat, son?'

'Only once,' said Scratchbelly. He shivered slightly. 'I'll have to do it, though. You'll have to point me in the right direction. In the

meantime, has anyone any suggestions on cat evasion?'

There was silence, broken eventually by a tentative cough. 'Yes, Number Three?'

'Well . . . um . . . it's just . . .' Number Three was clearly nervous; the cat problem was, essentially, his fault. 'You know the – um – the old saying: "A danger seen is a danger past." Well . . .'

'Go on,' said Scratchbelly kindly. Number Three continued more confidently.

'We're most at risk when we're looking for food – eating it or carrying it – because we can't concentrate completely on that and the cat at the same time. But if one of us went out on purpose to keep the cat busy, the rest could get on with foraging while he concentrated on cat-dodging.' He looked at their faces. 'You see, he'd be EXPECTING the cat. He'd have the advantage.'

There was a moment's silence. Then Scratchbelly said slowly, 'It's a good idea.

Brilliant, in fact.' Number Three swelled a little. 'But who is going to be this . . . this cat-bait?'

Number Three swallowed. 'It was my idea,' he said bravely. 'And the cat is here because of me. I'll have to do it.'

'Good lad,' said Scratchbelly warmly. The fact was that, had the young mouse not volunteered, Scratchbelly would have made him do it anyway: but he had shown a good spirit.

'Two things I ask,' said Number Three. 'First, that you don't forget to forage for me. Second' – he turned to his parents – 'when you name me, you were probably going to call me "Spotted" or "The Seen One" or something disgraceful. If I pull this off, can it be "Catmaster" or something like it, to be proud of?'

'Of course, dear,' said Slickwhiskers, before Scratchbelly could speak.

'Still no sign of Number Five,' he said irritably. 'Where's he got to?'

Number Five had got to the fireplace, triumphantly placed there by Hannibal.

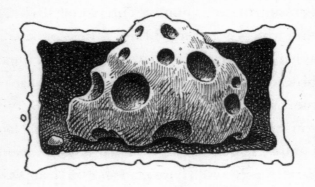

4

The death of Number Five increased the urgency of Scratchbelly's quest. But he could not leave immediately. The neighbouring family – the Flashfoot clan, so recently deprived of its leader – had to be told what was happening.

It was a cheerless visit. The Flashfoots were depressed and divided. There seemed to be a power struggle in progress between the two largest sons that was clearly uppermost in the minds of the whole family. They listened to Scratchbelly without comment or much apparent interest. One of the sons made a point of bringing up Number Three's disgrace in causing the situation; but none had any constructive suggestions.

'Well, I've done my best,' said Scratchbelly to Slickwhiskers when they were back in their own chamber, 'but they're a useless lot. They're not thinking straight. Hannibal's going to have them on toast.'

'Not if Number Three has anything to do with it,' said Slickwhiskers fondly. 'He's started already.'

As she spoke Number Three appeared in the chamber. He looked tired but proud as he went to the food left for him in the corner.

'That trapping cat – sorry Mum – that cat is no fool,' he said between mouthfuls. 'But I think I've got his measure. The trick is to be running for cover before he sees you. And I do a side-step at the last second which helps.'

Old Grey grunted. 'The running-for-cover is right,' he said gruffly. 'But I'd forget about the side-step if I was you. Remember: "shortest way will always pay." '

'I hope,' said Scratchbelly worriedly, 'that Hannibal doesn't realize what you're doing. If he does, he'll start looking over his shoulder when he sees you.'

'I know,' said Number Three. 'I've spoken to him a couple of times during the hole-wait. For a cat, he's not bad to talk to. But I'm pretending to be someone else each time, with a different name. And voice.'

'Excellent,' said Scratchbelly, his whiskers twitching in surprise. 'You're doing well. But don't pretend to be me – he's already met me.' Number Three is clearly a prospective Chief Mouse, he thought, provided he lasts long enough.

Number Three nodded. 'Well, back to it,' he said – then stopped in his tracks. The others froze. They could all hear the unmistakable accelerating thudding of the paws of a cat in full cry. The thudding grew louder, closer; at the entrance hole there was a muffled squeak, then a loud hissing sound, then silence. Scratchbelly waited for a moment, then left the chamber briefly.

'Hannibal,' he said heavily as he returned, 'has, at any rate, solved the Flashfoots' succession problem.'

'Sorry, Dad,' said Number Three mournfully. 'I should have been out there.'

'Not your fault,' said Scratchbelly gruffly. 'You've got to eat sometime. But the sooner I bring Hannibal a rat, the better. Come on, Old Grey. I need you to show me the way.'

'Before we go,' said Old Grey, 'I feel there are some things you should know.' He adopted the irritatingly professorial manner which he normally used for instructing young mice. 'I do have, after all, considerable experience.'

Scratchbelly sighed. Still, Old Grey might

know something useful. 'All right,' he said. 'Tell me about rats, for a start.'

'Rats, as you know if you have seen one, are much larger than us,' said Old Grey, 'but in many ways they are physically similar. They are rodents, after all. They are not, however, well-disposed to mice, generally speaking, and although they are not Predators, they may well kill a mouse in their territory. I think,' he scratched an ear pensively, 'they object to us sharing their food sources. I do not know how you plan to bring one here, but it will not be easy.'

Scratchbelly didn't have a plan but he wasn't going to let Old Grey know that. 'Thank you,' he said politely. 'Anything else?'

Old Grey settled back comfortably. 'Yes. The journey to the bottom of the garden is a long one,' he said, 'and all of it in the Open. Have you travelled in the Open, boy?'

Scratchbelly grunted. Apart from short-distance dashes along an outside wall – well screened by flowerpots and dead leaves – he had never been in the open air. The journey was a frightening prospect: resolutely, he put on a brave face.

'Very little,' he said. 'And you, Old Grey? I don't recall you going outside much.'

'Oh, I have been there,' said Old Grey. 'And my grandfather, he was a much-travelled mouse. You know, it was he who first settled on this house. He came from—'

'Yes, yes, we know, you've told us,' said Scratchbelly. '*Many* times,' murmured Slickwhiskers.

Old Grey continued regardless. 'My grandfather and father told me a lot that you need to know,' he said. 'First, this cat. If he sees you in the Open you are in deep trouble. Cover, of a sort, there is; but it is what is known as Soft Cover and is in any case usually too far away, unlike our walls which, because they give solid protection' – he looked sharply at Scratchbelly and Slickwhiskers to check on their attentiveness – 'are called Hard Cover, and usually we have a hole close at hand.'

'I don't think they let Hannibal out much,' said Slickwhiskers. 'Only in the early morning, to make dung.'

Scratchbelly gave a short laugh. 'From what Hannibal's told me,' he said, 'he's had quite enough of the Open. He won't come out unless he's kicked.'

'That's good,' said Old Grey. 'But there may be other cats. So you must use Soft Cover – leaves, bushes, grass – wherever possible and double-check the area if you have to cross open ground.'

'What other Predators are likely to be around?' Scratchbelly tried to sound casual.

'Well, dogs are fairly common,' said Old Grey. 'But they should not, in fact, present a problem.' He spoke with disdain. 'They are generally much bigger than cats but also much noisier: you should have no trouble hearing one coming. You may even have time to dig a hide-hole. And

I am told that certain dogs may be dodged if your footwork is neat enough. Unlike cats.'

'What about humans?' asked Slickwhiskers fearfully. 'I've seen them go outside into the garden.'

'Rarely in this season,' said Old Grey. 'And anyway, they will not see you, even if you're caught out of cover. We all know how poorly they see indoors: in the Open, they're even worse.'

'What else?' said Scratchbelly.

'On the ground, not much really,' Old Grey said in a slightly disappointed tone. 'You might meet a hedgehog. Bigger than us – about rat size – and very prickly, but fairly slow and not a Predator. Just keep out of its way and it'll leave you alone. There are some terrible things my grandfather spoke of called Stoats 'n' Weasels. I can tell you very little about them, never having seen one. Fortunately they are rarely encountered.' He abandoned his professorial tone abruptly. 'But if you do meet one, you're dead.'

Scratchbelly licked his lips nervously but said nothing.

'There is, however, another source of danger,' said Old Grey, going back into lecturing mode. 'I refer to the danger from On High.'

'What, you mean birds?' said Scratchbelly. 'Well, even *I*'ve seen birds. Little brown and grey jobs. One pecked at me once, just outside the wall. I gave it a mouthful. They don't seem to speak Mammal, but it got the message and cleared off, no trouble.'

'Sparrows,' said Old Grey scornfully. 'There are others. Most will not trouble you, but hide yourself nonetheless. Starlings and blackbirds are bigger and could seriously hurt you if they wanted to. The greater danger is hawks and owls. I have never seen an owl; but I have seen a hawk.' He shuddered and fell silent.

'What happened?' said Scratchbelly.

'It descends from On High,' said Old Grey quietly. 'There is nothing faster or more deadly than a hawk. Nothing. So,' pulling himself together, 'in addition to watching the ground, you must constantly check the sky. If you see a large bird high up, crouch and freeze. Do NOT run, even if you are in the open. If you make a move, I promise you it will be your last.' He fell silent.

'Anything else?' said Scratchbelly wearily.

'Nothing more that I can think of,' said Old Grey regretfully. He rose stiffly from his haunches. 'Come on. I'll set you on your way.'

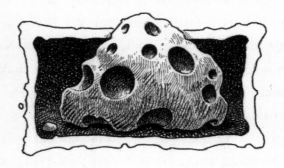

5

It did not take long to get outside, for the mice
were already in an outside wall. A few feet inside
the wall cavity, a sharp turn and a squeeze
through a crack in the foundations made by an
elder bush brought them momentarily on to a
concrete path. They crossed it in a flash. In the
safe cover of a berberis bush they faced each
other for a final parley.

'A short run along this border to the end of
it, turn right along another one,' said Old

Grey. 'There is a hedge next to the border and plenty of shrubs in the border itself. Good Soft Cover. I suggest you use the border for travelling and take to the hedge if danger appears. This will take you most of the way.'

'Sounds fine,' said Scratchbelly. 'Dead easy, in fact.'

'Or easy dead,' said Old Grey drily. 'Unfortunately, I said *most* of the way – not all. You will know when the long border ends because a stream cuts across it. You must follow the stream to the right.' He frowned. 'There is little cover there,' he said. 'The stream bank is too tidy. Stones and slabs on your left and lawn on your right. More cover on the lawn, but you may lose your direction; so I say, follow the slabs and take to the grass for hiding. You must also take care not to run into the rats unexpectedly, for they are often in this area. They live in bank-holes by the stream where the path ends.'

'Thank you, Old Grey,' said Scratchbelly.

They touched whiskers. 'I'll see you soon.'

Old Grey grunted, turned tail and was gone.

Scratchbelly waited a moment, reluctant to leave the friendly branches of the berberis. Then he drew a deep breath and set out.

The first part of the journey, though not without incident, was remarkably successful. At one point, Scratchbelly was seen by a blackbird perched on the hedge-top. It gave its deafening alarm call as it dropped to the lawn and pursued him into the hedge; then it lost interest and began worming in the border, which meant that he was stuck in the hedge for some time. And much later he was again scuttling for cover when a burst of barking from the far side of the hedge told him that some dog or other had seen or smelt him. The hedge was, thankfully, too thick for a dog to get through, and after another immobile session Scratchbelly went on his way.

The main trouble with the journey was its

length: not just the distance, but the time it took. Being ultra-cautious, Scratchbelly checked and double-checked the ground and the sky, selecting his next cover carefully and then dashing to it before repeating the process all over again. The blackbird and dog incidents added to his journey time; so did the need to feed. Fortunately there was food about – flower seeds mostly, including some dried sweet pea pods and some yarrow and poppy seeds.

The weak winter sun had been at its height when Scratchbelly started his journey, but by the time he reached the stream the shadow of the hedge was reaching on to the lawn. In the short term this very helpfully obscured him, but it also made Scratchbelly uneasy. In the house the dark was a friend but in the Open . . . it made him strangely nervous. He retreated to the shelter of the hedge to consider the terrain he had to cross.

The stream was in a deep cutting. A path of slabs set like stepping stones in the grass ran parallel with it on top of the cutting. The lawn spread away to the right, back towards the house. Scratchbelly could not see where the path ended. The slabs looked horribly bare and exposed. The lawn was better but not much: it was mown short and the yellowing grass offered minimal cover.

Scratchbelly moved a few feet along the hedge to where it ended above the stream and examined the bank. Rocks and large stones were set into it rockery-fashion. There were some plants between them but also a good deal of bare earth. The rocks were too exposed for Scratchbelly's liking but they threw some shadow, and the plants would be useful. As a route, he decided, the bank was definitely preferable to the path or the lawn. Better still, he found that by going well down, close to the water, he was often in the shadow of the rocks above and there was a certain amount of long grass and even some flag-irises to provide shelter. Even so there were several nerve-racking lengthy stretches in the Open and some uncomfortable rock climbing to endure. Scratchbelly felt himself becoming nervously and physically exhausted. So much so that he had almost forgotten about the rats; it was only sheer good fortune that prevented him running right into them. He had paused behind a large, damp stone at the water's edge and was just about to restart when a movement on the opposite bank caught his eye. Immediately he crouched and watched.

The ground on the other side of the stream rose less steeply. The low bank was topped by a tall wooden fence. The movement – a mere twitching of grass at the base of the fence – was repeated further down the bank, and the rat broke cover at the water's edge.

Scratchbelly knew rats were big but he hadn't reckoned on them being this big. The rat was carrying a large lump of what seemed to be bread in its mouth, displaying menacing yellow teeth in the process. Its feet, too, were

intimidating. It paced steadily along the bank bottom, paused for a moment and leapt lazily on to a large stone in the middle of the stream. Another leap and it was on the same side as Scratchbelly, still just visible but moving smartly away in front of him.

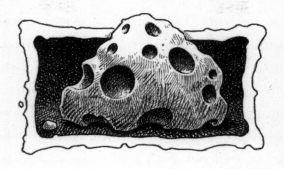

6

Scratchbelly gulped. Instinctively he wanted to turn and run as fast as possible back home; but he had to bring a rat with him and to do that he had to contact one. He had gone only a few feet when the grass by the fence stirred again and he dived for the shelter of his stone. Another rat appeared, also carrying food – this time a decaying piece of apple – and it followed the same course as the first. Even as Scratchbelly watched it jump from the stone in the stream, a third rat appeared on the opposite bank. Like the first, it was carrying bread, but for some reason it decided to ignore the route via the stone and instead swim the short distance across the stream, coming almost straight for Scratchbelly, who quickly pressed himself to the earth. He kept one eye exposed round the side of his stone and prepared himself for instant flight, but the rat turned and marched beneath him, following the others. It was perilously close. The bread it carried was, Scratchbelly noted, decidedly mouldy and covered with pinkish and blue-grey patches. They certainly have a plentiful food source, Scratchbelly thought, but the quality is very poor indeed . . . and suddenly, he had a plan.

Scratchbelly broke cover and set off in pursuit of the rat, abandoning caution in his desire to catch it up. This was not easy. The rat was much bigger and faster. It covered the ground rapidly,

leaving Scratchbelly scrambling over rocks at
full speed without noticeably gaining on
his quarry – but at least he could see it.
Until, that is, the rat approached a large
boulder and suddenly dropped down the bank.
It had disappeared into a cunningly hidden
entrance hole in the boulder's overhang.

Concealed by a clump of long, yellowish
grass, Scratchbelly regained his breath and
considered his next move. As he studied the
entrance a slight movement on the boulder
above it revealed yet another rat. This one was
much larger than those Scratchbelly had seen
so far; a huge creature with a light sandy-
coloured coat. Hidden from above by some
dropping frost-browned irises, the rat stood
motionless on the rock, gazing down the track
where Scratchbelly lay and occasionally turning
his head to look over the stream or to his rear.
Clearly he was there to watch for danger and
give the alarm: almost certainly he was the
Chief Rat.

They're well prepared, thought Scratchbelly, much more organized than us. He shivered with fear at what he was going to do; but there was no help for it if his plan was to succeed.

He left his hiding place and went with what he hoped was a carefree air towards the rat-hole, looking to left and right but taking care not to look at the big rat on the boulder.

Suddenly there was an excruciating pain in his right ear as he felt himself lifted by it, flicked over and deposited stomach-upward on the stone. The rat released his ear, only to place its jaws immediately across his throat.

'You are going to die,' he said coolly. 'Whether you die quick or slow depends on whether you tell me why you are here and who is with you.'

'I . . . I'm sorry,' said Scratchbelly humbly. 'I'm alone. I come from the house. I got lost in the garden and – well, I saw one of you carrying some kind of food which I had never seen before. I followed to get a closer look and you grabbed me. I know it was foolish but I did not realize I was on your territory.'

The rat bared its teeth. 'It was very foolish, but you will not make the same mistake again. Or any other mistakes.' He frowned suddenly. 'This food – you say the last rat down was carrying it? That was bread. Don't tell me you've never seen dogging bread.'

Acutely aware of the rat's teeth at his neck, Scratchbelly replied carefully, 'This was coloured. Pink, blue, green, grey – I've never seen coloured bread.'

The rat stared at him. 'Mould,' he said. 'It was mouldy bread!'

'I have never seen it before,' said Scratchbelly, trying to look innocent. 'All the bread I've seen is white. Not that I eat it often,' he gabbled, buying time. 'There *is* bread of course, lots of it, but there is so much other stuff to choose from that I rarely bother with it. Raisins and cheese are so much more tasty, don't you think?'

The rat's grip loosened slightly and Scratchbelly felt his neck-fur dampened by saliva. 'You say you come from the house?' the rat said. 'You get these foods – from the house?'

'Where else?' said Scratchbelly. 'It is there for the taking. There are humans there of course, but they do not trouble us. There is so much, I don't think they notice what we take.'

The rat sat back for a moment, then lunged forward swiftly and grabbed Scratchbelly's undamaged left ear. But it did not close its jaws fully.

'I think,' said the rat, 'that we shall not kill you just yet. The Chief may be interested in what you've told me. Answer his questions truthfully, do exactly what he tells you, and you may even survive.'

As he spoke he dropped from the boulder, dragging Scratchbelly painfully with him, and slid rapidly into the hole.

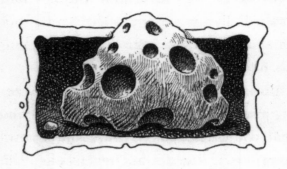

7

Scratchbelly was pulled along so quickly
that he was unable to take in much. In spite
of his predicament he felt relieved to be
underground, out of the Open at last. There
were several tunnels joining the entrance one:
clearly this was a complex Rattery which he
would be unable to escape from unaided. Used
to the cramped but dry runs in the house, he
found the tunnels unpleasantly high and dank.
The rat-smell was overpowering.

As the rat moved deeper into the Rattery Scratchbelly was aware of a slight relaxation of his jaws and a slowing, almost a hesitation, in his pace. Suddenly they stopped and Scratchbelly was pulled roughly through a right angle into a side hole which opened out into a small chamber. A rat sat there with his back to them, eating from a pile of brownish bits of apple. He looked over his shoulder at them.

'Ah, Gromuncho,' said the rat. 'And what is this' – with a jab of a forefoot at Scratchbelly – 'doing here?'

He was nowhere near as big as Gromuncho, nor so distinctively coloured; but there was no doubt in Scratchbelly's mind that *this* was the Chief Rat. There was an evident intelligence and composure about him; and then there were his eyes, which gleamed with unusual brilliance and were focused, with almost cat-like binocular vision, on Scratchbelly. The eyes then focused on Gromuncho, and Scratchbelly sensed the big rat's unease.

'I hope you have a good reason for this, Gromuncho,' said the Chief Rat. 'You know the standing order – all mice, voles and other small rodents found near the Rattery to be killed and either eaten or disposed of behind the Fence. So, why not this one?'

Gromuncho did his best to hide his nervousness. 'He has some . . . some important information, Chief. Comes from the house. Says that the food there is plentiful, easy to get and fresh. So much of it and so fresh he didn't know what mouldy bread looked like. I thought we . . . I mean, I thought *you* might want to investigate it.'

The Chief Rat looked at him for a moment longer, then suddenly switched his piercing gaze to Scratchbelly. 'Is this true, mouse?' The voice was quiet but horribly menacing. Scratchbelly had no difficulty in sounding fearful.

'Yes sir,' he said miserably. 'We feed very well, and have no trouble getting food. I wish it wasn't so, now – otherwise I wouldn't be here.

I went for a stroll to walk down a good feed of sweetcorn, got lost and ended up here. I wish' – he sighed heavily – 'I wish I hadn't.'

'You say, no trouble getting it,' said the Chief Rat. 'Don't the humans object?'

'They aren't there much and they see nothing. You know how blind humans are, and these are probably extra stupid.' Scratchbelly tried to laugh nervously.

'Is there no cat?'

Scratchbelly had already decided on his reply to this. It might be that the rats had already seen Hannibal.

'There is a cat,' he said carelessly, 'but he gives no trouble. Spends most of his time asleep on a bed upstairs. He's very fat and slow and I don't think he knows much about mousing.'

The Chief Rat was silent for a moment. 'We know the house,' he said at length. 'We have considered exploring it but could find no way in. Is there' – the eyes burned even brighter – 'a rat's way in?'

This was the tricky moment. It would not do to be *too* helpful. Both of them knew that a rat invasion would be disastrous for the mouse community. Scratchbelly swallowed. This was going to call for some acting. He spoke a little too loudly, too deliberately.

'There is n-no way in for a rat.'

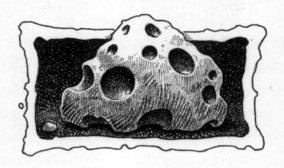

8

The rat's muzzle was thrust against Scratchbelly's nose. 'Think again,' he said, lifting his lip to bare ferocious teeth. His blazing eyes bored into Scratchbelly's. 'Think very carefully. Is there a rat's way in?'

Scratchbelly withheld his answer for a second or two, pretending to struggle between fear and duty.

'There is perhaps a way in,' he said reluctantly. 'But you would never find it.'

The rat's muzzle remained on Scratchbelly's for a moment. Then the glare from his eyes softened and the rat drew back.

'You have done well, Gromuncho,' he said, without warmth. Scratchbelly felt the big rat behind him relax and heard his quiet sigh of relief. 'This certainly warrants investigation. You will go to the house with this mouse immediately. He will show you the way in.' Scratchbelly started appropriately. 'Oh yes you will,' the rat said to him. 'If you do not – if you fail to cooperate in any way – Gromuncho will kill you very painfully and slowly. No doubt you are hungry. You will be fed before the journey.'

Scratchbelly was decidedly hungry, but he caught himself just in time. 'I am in no need of food,' he said. 'I was bloated when I set out and am still pretty full. But a drink would be nice. I am very thirsty.'

'Take him to the stream, Gromuncho,' said the Chief Rat. 'You will then set out with him immediately to the house, investigate the inside and report back to me as soon as possible.'

Scratchbelly felt Gromuncho's tension return like an electric shock. 'What, now?' said the big rat. 'But . . . Grabblo, the sun is nearly down. Wouldn't it be better to wait till morning? Surely you don't want me to go now?'

The Chief Rat's eyes blazed again. 'You disappoint me, Gromuncho,' he said icily. 'You bring me important news. That is good, most meritorious. Now I am offering you a chance to make a real name for yourself. If the outcome is successful we shall have better food, even an extension of the Rattery. Your prestige will be very high. And you are dithering? Afraid to go? This news is too important to wait for, Gromuncho. I don't countenance delay – or fear. If you are refusing to go I can find others more eager. So, stay if you wish. But your refusal will be noted. And' – he spoke lower, a hissing whisper – 'it will certainly be made public.'

Gromuncho was still quivering behind

Scratchbelly, but he answered firmly enough. 'Sorry, Grabblo,' he said. 'Stupid of me. I'll go of course. Be back in no time, don't worry.'

'I am not worrying,' said the Chief Rat calmly. 'Take the mouse to drink and be on your way. Take the direct route across the lawn, for speed. And now you must excuse me, I have a matter to attend to with one of the youngsters.' He came towards them, forcing them to reverse into the main tunnel, then paused in the entrance. 'Good luck, Gromuncho.'

Gromuncho cuffed Scratchbelly into motion. He no longer held the mouse's ear, contenting himself with remaining close behind him and tapping him to turn him left or right into the correct route. In a very short time they emerged a few inches above the level of the stream, hidden by some bramble-covered bricks. The terrain was unfamiliar to Scratchbelly: it must, he concluded, be some way beyond the entrance where he had been apprehended. He decided to try a little conversation.

'Very convenient, this,' he said brightly, 'but doesn't the hole flood when the stream rises?'

'Shut up and drink,' said his companion shortly. Scratchbelly noticed that the big rat was scanning the sky anxiously. The sun had set. The sky was clear and the glow from the west was still bright, but eastwards the night was encroaching fast. He drank long and gratefully, and managed surreptitiously to swallow a few mouthfuls of water-weed before a sharp jerk on his tail brought him back to the hole.

'Now get a move on,' said Gromuncho, and drove him back through the Rattery at a great pace. Eventually they emerged high up the stream bank and moved to the top of it. Scratchbelly recognized the stepping-stone slabbed path which ran above the bank, and the open lawn beyond it. Far away in the distance, the house lights glowed comfortably.

'Go,' snapped Gromuncho, 'and go fast. And remember, I'm right behind you so no tricks.' He bit the mouse's tail suddenly, for emphasis.

Scratchbelly sprang across the path and on to the lawn. The grass was hopelessly short, useless as cover, unpleasantly damp and bitterly cold, for the clear air was already crackling with frost. He went blindly forward. It was impossible to maintain the pace, of course, although Gromuncho gave him no respite, cursing, cuffing and biting him to keep him on course and up to speed. He was soon exhausted and there was a long way to go. Fortunately Gromuncho had not totally abandoned caution and occasionally called 'Freeze!' suddenly when some noise or movement alarmed him. Scratchbelly was glad to suck air into his lungs at each brief pause.

The moon rose and bathed the lawn in whiteness. We must stand out like currants in a bun, thought Scratchbelly, desperately scampering with Gromuncho's shadow visible out of the corner of his eye. And yet he felt strangely elated. In spite of all the risks his plan was working: he was bringing a rat

for Hannibal. If he could just get across this lawn . . .

Suddenly the moon went out.

Without thought, Scratchbelly stopped dead, flattened himself to the earth and clamped his eyes shut. There was a strange sound like a gentle muffled roar behind him, then a piercing squeal and finally two brief surges of air over his motionless body. He remained stock-still for at least a minute, then opened an eye. The moon was shining down again and all was silent. But Gromuncho had disappeared.

For a second he stood perplexed: then panic took over. He knew only that he must get off this awful, white lawn; he could not get to the house or back to the stream without a lengthy journey and he was tired, but he must, must get to Cover.

He was within an ace of running blindly in circles when he remembered the hedge and border which had protected him on the way down. Of course! Desperately he tore off to the right. Yes, there it was. His lungs heaved and his feet slipped on the icy turf, but the border was getting nearer. He paused for breath and dashed again . . . Traps and cats! It should be closer by now. He repeated the pause and the dash; repeated it again. And again. Would he never get there? And then, suddenly, the lawn edge was before him and he tumbled gratefully into the border under a sage bush.

'You can come out,' said a familiar voice from the hedge bottom. 'All clear.'

Scratchbelly looked up. The eyes of Grabblo the Chief Rat shone back at him.

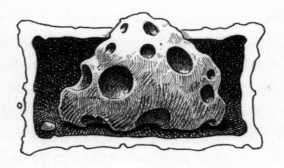

9

'You seem surprised to see me,' said the rat. 'It was necessary that I be on hand when the owl took Gromuncho. I have been following your progress from the cover of the border.'

'So . . . it was an owl?' said Scratchbelly. 'I never saw it, but I heard it – a sort of roar, and then a squeal.'

'The squeal was Gromuncho,' said Grabblo. 'And owls do not roar. They often screech when they attack, and hoot sometimes, but never roar. No doubt it was the sound of the wind through its wings. You are lucky. Not many hear it and live. But I did not think that, given the choice, the owl would prefer you to Gromuncho. He was a more substantial meal.'

'You mean,' said Scratchbelly slowly, 'you knew that the owl would come?'

'Of course. I brought it.'

'BROUGHT it?'

'Not difficult.' Grabblo spoke matter-of-factly. 'I simply went on to the lawn while you were drinking. Walked about, not too far from cover, so any owl would see me. There are always owls about at dusk – as Gromuncho well knew. I was in no danger because I was expecting an attack.' (Scratchbelly remembered, for an instant, Number Three's campaign against Hannibal.) 'So, when an owl turned up and came for me I skipped into the hedge with time to spare. But I knew he'd be back.'

'I don't understand,' said Scratchbelly, his fear of the Chief Rat momentarily overcome by curiosity. 'Are you saying that you wanted the owl to take Gromuncho? One of your own rats?'

'My Rattery is well-run and successful,' said Grabblo. He was talking as much to himself as to the mouse. 'We are well-concealed and have a good food supply from the compost heap behind the Fence. But we are only safe if the Humans are unaware of our presence. This is only possible if my rats keep strictly to my rules on routes and general behaviour. I have been necessarily severe on this. Unfortunately not all of them accept this necessity.' He bared his teeth in irritation. 'Gromuncho was one such. A fool. A big fool. He had the support of other malcontents. He would have challenged me before long. In combat he would undoubtedly have the advantage: not only bigger, but younger. So combat was to be avoided. Your arrival gave me the chance to get rid of him.'

'I see,' said Scratchbelly. 'And so . . . I suppose you no longer have any use for me?'

'On the contrary,' said Grabblo grimly. 'You interest me greatly. I tell you, mouse, I do not for one minute believe your story. So now' – he lunged forward and seized Scratchbelly's foreleg in his jaws – 'you will tell me the real reason for coming to me.'

Scratchbelly thought fast. He could not, of course, tell the rat the true reason for his journey. For a second he considered an alternative story – but that was no good. He didn't have one for a start; and Grabblo would be sure to spot any further attempts at lying. He decided to stick to his guns.

'I told you the truth,' he said aggrievedly. 'Why don't you believe me?'

'You went for a stroll,' said the rat contemptuously. 'House mice do not go for strolls in the Open. They hate the Open. I set watchers from time to time to observe the garden. They have never reported seeing house mice. Field mice and voles occasionally; a rabbit once; never a house mouse.'

'Nevertheless, I did go for a stroll,' said Scratchbelly stoutly. 'And it was not the first time, although today I went further than I meant to. You must realize, our situation is unusual. We have so much food and need make almost no effort to get it. This makes us fat and lazy, and also very bored.'

'You are not so fat,' said Grabblo.

'Because I take exercise – go for strolls,' said Scratchbelly patiently. 'Because we are bored, there is a lot of arguing and fighting. Well, if I am to fight I must be fit. I intend to win, you see: I intend to be Chief Mouse.' This was an inspired afterthought. He felt pleased with himself: Grabblo would surely fall for that.

The rat looked at him quizzically. 'Maybe,' he said at last. 'I am not entirely convinced but – maybe. But one thing is sure: you will never be a Chief Mouse. After you have taken me into the house your clan will kill you for bringing me, for there will be no room for you mice. We shall kill or drive out all of you. But you know this already, of course.'

'I know it,' said Scratchbelly heavily.

'Move on then. We shall, naturally, follow the border. Only a fool like Gromuncho would obey an order to cross the lawn in these conditions.'

They set off. Scratchbelly was still obliged to hurry, although Grabblo was moving at a relaxed rat-pace. The long trek was uneventful. Scratchbelly's legs were aching but he hardly noticed. His worries were mounting with each step. First he had to get the rat into the house. After that he would have to rely on fast-talking – and luck.

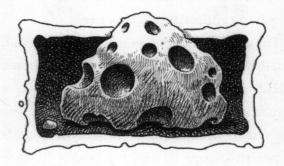

10

At last they arrived at the berberis where Scratchbelly had sheltered before setting out. Across the path, the stunted elder bush signalled the mouse-entrance to the house. Scratchbelly turned to his companion.

'My way in is there,' he said, pointing, 'but it is much too small for you. There is a way for you to enter, but I shall have to go in first to – er . . . arrange things to let you in.'

He felt that this sounded very thin. Clearly

Grabblo did too, for immediately the rat's teeth dropped on the back of his neck.

'Do not take me for a fool,' said Grabblo quietly. 'Now – you take me in, or my teeth meet.'

'It's not that easy,' Scratchbelly said desperately. 'The only way I know for you to enter is by the landing window. We shall have to push this open from the inside for you. It will take more than one of us.'

'Where is this window?'

'You go up the drainpipe – there – which runs past the window ledge. Jump from pipe to ledge. The window will be pushed outward; you go in underneath.' Scratchbelly paused. 'It is a journey for a rat, not a mouse: the climb is too long and the jump to the ledge too far for me. For you, no problem.'

Grabblo seemed to consider this; then, 'Very well,' he said. 'Call your friends out here.'

'They will not hear me from here. Even if they did, they might not come.'

The rat gave a short laugh. 'I am sure they

would not. So. You and I shall go to your hole together.'

They crossed the path. As they reached the hole Scratchbelly felt his tail clamped firmly.

'Now you will enter the hole,' said Grabblo. 'You will call the other mice to you and arrange for the window to be opened. Any nonsense and I shall pull you out and kill you.' He tightened his jaws on the mouse's tail.

Scratchbelly moved gingerly through the crack. He was able to turn slightly before a painful jerk on his tail told him that he could go no further. He called tremulously: 'Anybody about?'

At once there was a sound of movement and Number Three came rushing down the run at a great pace.

'Dad, you're back! Great! Did you bring the—?'

'We have a guest,' said Scratchbelly loudly. 'He is waiting outside. Unfortunately the entrance is too small for him. We must arrange

things so that he can join us.' As he spoke he
gestured fiercely with his forefeet to try to
explain his predicament. Number Three gazed
at him, totally uncomprehending. Desperately
Scratchbelly made 'turn round' signs to him.
Number Three was still bemused but turned
obediently. At once Scratchbelly grabbed his
tail between his teeth and pulled, gesturing
over his shoulder. Number Three gave a

70

short squawk and turned angrily. Seeing the gesture, he responded at first with a blank look. Scratchbelly repeated it, covering his mouth with the other paw to indicate silence. At last, Number Three understood, and nodded.

'What must we do, Father?' he said loudly – and, Scratchbelly felt, unconvincingly.

'Go to the landing window and make sure it is open. Take others with you to help.'

'Yes, Father. At once,' said Number Three in a piercing tenor. And set off at high speed in the wrong direction.

Scratchbelly choked back a shout to bring him back, shrugged and reversed slightly to relieve his tail-ache and speak to Grabblo.

'They are checking the window for you,' he said miserably. 'When they report back, you can come in.'

'Good,' said the rat. 'While we are waiting, I think I'll have you back out here with me. Just in case you feel like sacrificing your tail for freedom.' He jerked his head sharply and

Scratchbelly flew painfully backwards into the open air.

'They may be a little while,' he said nervously. The rat did not release his tail and made no answer. Time passed.

'Your friends are taking too long,' said Grabblo eventually. 'Explain that I have a hold on you, so to speak, and that things will be very painful for you if— Yow!' He gave a sudden surprised yell of pain – and dropped the tail. Scratchbelly was motionless for a split-second, stupefied by the unexpected noise, then came to his senses and whisked into the hole like lightning. Immediately he turned to look outside, in time to see Grabblo rushing down the path close behind a small brown figure which zig-zagged desperately in its efforts to escape. They disappeared and then came a mighty clattering from just outside the wall. Then silence. And then the sound of a scampering mouse – inside the wall. Number Three appeared, very breathless.

'Got – the message,' he said between pants. 'Went out – by conservatory drain. Attacked – from rear. Bit him – on the bum.'

'Thank you, Number Three,' said Scratchbelly. It was all there was time to say. 'Now – get Hannibal! Get him to the stairs! We let the rat in and – the job's done.'

'Bit of a problem there,' said Number Three. 'Was going to tell you but – didn't get the chance. You see, Dad – Hannibal's gone!'

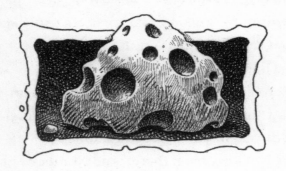

11

Scratchbelly stared at him. 'What do you mean – gone?'

'They took him away earlier. In a basket. He didn't want to go. Lots of bad language. The Male took him. I guess,' said Number Three dolefully, 'I did too well. He didn't catch enough of us so they've sent him back.'

Scratchbelly groaned; then, as realization dawned, dashed down the run, calling to his son to follow – only to run full tilt into

Slickwhiskers, Old Grey and three of the Flashfoot clan who had heard the noise of Number Three's escape and were arriving somewhat belatedly to investigate.

'Come with me!' yelled Scratchbelly, charging past them and rocketing out of the first exit hole, which brought him underneath the dining-room sideboard. Throwing caution to the wind he dashed across the room and under the door into the hall. Only when he had reached the foot of the stairs did he stop to wait for the others. They joined him quickly enough, although Old Grey was well behind the rest and clearly suffering from his exertions.

'The landing window,' panted Scratchbelly. 'Is it open?'

'Sure to be,' said Slickwhiskers. 'They always leave it open a crack. Don't ask me why, in the middle of winter. Stupid I always think, when it's so cold . . .'

'Never mind that,' snapped Scratchbelly. 'We've got to get there fast. We can't shut the window, but, if there are enough of us, we can stop him getting in. Fight him off.'

'Stop who?' said one of the Flashfoots.

'We've got a chance,' said Number Three, springing on to the first step. 'I led him into some flowerpots – made a hell of a noise. He probably had to freeze for a bit. Let's go.'

But it was not a quick journey. There were a dozen steps to the landing, each of them an exhausting jump and climb. The mice made the best speed they could. Scratchbelly repeatedly looked upward, hoping against hope that they were in time to defeat Grabblo.

They had reached the top step and were about to scale the landing chair to reach the sill when a scratching and a light thud above them told Scratchbelly that they were too late. He looked up. Grabblo peered over the edge of the sill, his eyes burning malevolently down.

'Better late than never,' said Grabblo sarcastically. 'As you can see, I was able to push my way in without your help. But then, you were not coming to help, were you? No. Now, after all, I shall see for myself this bounteous plenty you spoke of. But first – some punishment is in order. I promised to kill you, mouse, if you tricked me. I do not renege on promises.'

As he spoke he sprang from the sill towards Scratchbelly. Scratchbelly flung himself desperately from the landing into space. He had a brief view of Old Grey looking up at him from under the top step before he struck the lip of the step below, flew through the air again and landed upright four steps down. Desperately he leapt on downwards, dimly aware of the other mice fleeing in panic beside and behind him, and of the heavier-footed pursuit of the Chief Rat.

In truth it was no contest, for the rat's leaps were many times longer than anything a mouse could produce. Grabblo and Scratchbelly reached the hall floor together, the rat's jaws scything at his prey in mid-leap. Scratchbelly dodged and sprinted – but there was no hole, no rat-proof cover to run to. The rat sprang, mouth open; Scratchbelly felt the teeth skim his flank, leapt and dodged again. He was trapped in the middle of the hall now; Grabblo had him, and they both knew it. The other mice were grouped near the dining-room door, watching in dismay. Grabblo crouched ready for a final spring; then paused and addressed them, never taking his eyes off Scratchbelly.

'I shall now kill you,' he said calmly. 'Later, I shall bring other rats here, through the window which you have so kindly shown me. It will be better for the rest of you if you leave now rather than later.'

Slickwhiskers spoke nervously. 'How do you know it will be worth it here? There is not much food. And we have a cat.'

'Where is this cat?' said the rat contemptuously. 'As to the food – there is always food in houses, if you can get in to find it. We shall come and we shall stay. So move out or die, as this one is about to do.'

He bared his teeth for a final lunge – then
jerked upright as a crash of breaking glass came
from the landing above. Scratchbelly looked
up. A slender flower-vase which normally stood
on the landing window-sill had gone.

In its place, far above him, he could just
make out the figure of Old Grey. And then
from the sitting-room came the heavy,
thumping tread of Human feet. The door next
to the stairs flew open and, with a click, the hall
was flooded with dazzling light.

The watching mice disappeared promptly under the dining-room door. Scratchbelly had nowhere to run to, and froze. The Female Human never saw him. But she certainly saw Grabblo.

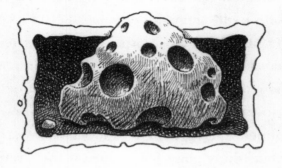

12

Things happened quickly after that.

There was a deafening shriek from the Human. The sound was so loud that Scratchbelly was momentarily stunned. Grabblo looked round for escape. All the hall doors except the one where the Human stood were closed and too well-fitting for a rat to go underneath. He glanced up at the stairs and shook his head briefly; he would never make it back to the window and in any case he could only get through it by wriggling. He did the only thing possible: went straight for the open door into the sitting-room.

The Human gave another deafening screech and disappeared through the doorway, pursued by the darting rat. Scratchbelly's curiosity overcame caution. He followed, rounded the door-edge – and leapt skyward as a huge shiny glass object meant for Grabblo came skimming across the carpet and smashed into the door. Scratchbelly leapt over the remains of the ashtray and took cover under a small cabinet to view the proceedings.

The rat advanced to the centre of the room and jumped on to a footstool to view the options and consider his next move. The Female Human stood at the far end. She held a rolled-up magazine but seemed nervous and uncertain about attacking. Grabblo had sensed this and was going through an impressive variety of snarls and snorts, making a great play with his bared teeth.

Scratchbelly knew the room well, naturally.

He was starting to worry. There was no rat-way out, he knew – except one. The room had a fireplace. The chimney would give the rat shelter – but, worse still, it would give him a way into the wall, via a loose brick a few feet up. Then Grabblo would have the freedom of the cavities where the mice lived.

The rat was looking round the room steadily. Then his gaze fastened, as Scratchbelly had feared, on the fireplace.

'Hope he doesn't get in there,' said Number Three's voice in Scratchbelly's ear.

'You shouldn't be here,' said Scratchbelly, but only half-heartedly: he was glad of the company.

'Needed to see where he goes,' said Number Three, 'so we can act accordingly.'

Scratchbelly grunted. Number Three was taking a lot on himself. But this was no time to argue. He watched the rat. Fortunately the Female Human had accidentally taken up a position in front of the fireplace. Grabblo glared at her and dropped deliberately to the floor, then moved step by step towards her. She waved the magazine ineffectually; Scratchbelly sensed that she would not block Grabblo's way for long. Grabblo sensed it too; Scratchbelly saw his back legs tense, ready for a sharp, straight dash to the fireplace – then an unexpected commotion brought his head snapping round towards the door.

Scratchbelly heard it too: the familiar squeak and bang of the front door. A moment later the Male Human came into the room. He was bleeding from a long scratch on his cheek; and in his arms he held the struggling form of Hannibal.

The Female Human shrieked again. The Male stood astonished, trying to take in the situation. Hannibal took it in very much faster. With an angry yowl he sprang from the Human's arms and streaked across the room. Grabblo saw his chance and darted for the safety of the fireplace, bringing another scream and a hurried retreat from the Female. He had reached the firebasket when Hannibal, at full stretch, knocked him sideways with a last-ditch swing of his right paw. The rat rolled over on to the tiled surround and sprang back, spitting. But his fate was sealed. Hannibal crouched between him and safety.

There was no denying, as Scratchbelly said afterwards, that the Chief Rat put up a good fight. He immediately went on the offensive, dashing towards a surprised Hannibal, leaping and slashing with open jaws. Hannibal recoiled and cursed horribly as the rat's teeth ripped his front leg. Many a cat would have retreated; but Hannibal was clearly rat-experienced. His big rear-leg muscles contracted. Grabblo rose on his back legs, ready to dodge the expected high spring and pounce. It never came. Instead Hannibal dived forward, keeping low. Claws and teeth struck almost simultaneously. Grabblo was thrown on to his back and died instantly.

* * *

The cat remained in the killing position for a full half-minute. Then the long black body relaxed and Hannibal stood up. With a casual flick of the head he sent the rat's body rolling on to the fireplace tiles and stalked slowly to the centre of the room.

'Big show-off,' said Number Three admiringly.

The Humans, who had been standing stock-still since Hannibal's intervention, now burst into life. Hannibal was picked up and hugged and stroked to an accompanying roar of endearments and praises. The cat purred as required, although the mice were able to hear his real thoughts in the purring. 'All right, all right! Give over! If you really want to do me a favour, dish out some grub!'

Scratchbelly and Number Three came out from their hiding place and slipped towards the door. The Humans, they knew, were too engrossed to spot them. But the Female had lifted Hannibal on to her shoulder, and he saw them.

For a second his eyes widened. The mice watched apprehensively. Then Hannibal gave a tiny shake of the head and the eyes closed.

Next morning, Scratchbelly, recovering from a hearty celebratory meal in the main chamber, was disturbed by the arrival of one of the young mice from the Flashfoot clan. He came in tentatively and cowered respectfully.

'Excuse me, sir, but – the cat wants to speak to you.'

'Thank you,' said Scratchbelly, trying to sound as if this was quite the usual thing. 'Where is he?'

'By the hole in the fireplace. Thank you, sir,' said the youngster, and disappeared.

Scratchbelly worked his way along the passageways and climbed up to the loose brick. 'Hannibal?'

'Ah, there you are,' said the cat. 'Just to say, thanks very much. That was quite a rat you brought me. No chance of another one I suppose?'

'No,' said Scratchbelly emphatically. 'Definitely not. No chance at all. And anyway, where were you to start with? It nearly did for me, you not being there.'

'They were taking me back to the farm – which was your fault, or rather that young mouse's fault. Put me in a dogging cardboard box.' Hannibal twitched his tail irritably at the memory. 'Well, I wasn't having that. Just tore the bottom out of it and jumped around a bit. Of course, we were in the car by then. The Male tried to catch me but I scratched him a bit – not deep, you understand, but enough to get him to turn round and come back. You must admit my timing was pretty good.'

'You were nearly too late. Anyway, it seems to have worked. You're the big hero.'

'I have eaten,' said Hannibal, rolling slowly on to his back, 'an entire tin of Kittymeat and a large piece of fish, and they have given me two saucers of milk. What's more, the Male brought in a big boxful of Kittymeat tins this morning. I think I have it made. I'm going to be a fat cat.'

'That's good. For us, I trust, as well as you.'

'Yes,' said Hannibal. 'Mind you, don't go taking liberties. If one of your youngsters runs across my nose, I'll have him. I'm still a cat, and don't you forget it.'

'That's understood,' said Scratchbelly.

'Talking of youngsters,' said Hannibal, 'who's the young dare-devil that's been giving me the runaround? Got a death wish, but he's smart.'

'Oh, we have lots of smart youngsters,' said Scratchbelly innocently.

'Don't give me that,' said the cat. 'He's been trying to fool me with different names and voices. But it's the same mouse all right. I know by that silly side-step he always does when he gets to the hole. Someone should tell him to drop that.'

'He hasn't got a name yet,' said Scratchbelly. 'As a matter of fact, we've got to give him one very soon.'

'I have a name for him – OK if I name him?'

'We would be honoured if you named him,' said Scratchbelly after an astonished pause. 'A cat naming a mouse – it's never happened before.'

'Then I name him Sidestepper,' said Hannibal. He stood and stretched luxuriously. 'And now I must be going. I hear the sound of a tin of Kittymeat being opened for breakfast. Be seeing you.'

'Not if I see you first,' said Scratchbelly politely.

Part II

1

Hannibal the cat thrust his shoulder into the corner of the door and eased his long black body round the edge of it and into the sitting-room. He paused for a moment to survey his surroundings, then paced slowly with head held low, panther-fashion, across the sunlit carpet to the fireplace rug and settled smoothly on to it. He gazed fixedly at the fireplace and called quietly – too quietly for detection by a human ear.

There was a tiny skittering from the fireplace.

'That you, Scratchbelly?' said the cat.

'Good morning, Hannibal,' said the mouse, gazing safely down at him from the break in the chimney brickwork just above the fireplace mouth. 'How are you? Fat and well, by the look of you. Your belly covers more of that rug every time I see you.'

But Hannibal was clearly not in the mood for pleasantries.

'Look here,' he said crossly. 'You did me a favour and in return I've left you lot alone. A bit of respect isn't too much to ask for, is it? I don't need to catch mice and don't particularly want to – at least, not you and Sidestepper.' He looked away, slightly bashful. 'It is nice to have someone to talk to, I admit – the Humans never understand a word I say.' Then the angry tone returned abruptly. 'But fair's fair. If you take liberties with me, the deal's off. I still have my reputation to think of.'

'Oh dear. What's happened?' said Scratchbelly, dropping his jovial tone.

'One of your young mice walked over my front foot when I was dozing at the bottom of the stairs. Stepped over it, said, "Hello Blackbum", and walked off giggling. Very irritating. I put the claws out but just managed to hold back; thought I'd speak to you first. But it's the last time. Any more of it and I start tasting mouse again.'

'What did he look like?' said Scratchbelly wearily. 'No, don't bother, I'll tell you. One ear curled over, black spot on the side of his nose and rolls when he walks?'

'You've got him,' said the cat.

'Nutcruncher's Number Seven,' said Scratchbelly with a sigh. He was silent for a moment; then, with exasperation, continued: 'Oh look, for goodness' sake have him. Nutcruncher Seven is nothing but bad news. He's bound to be Spotted, then we'll all be in trouble. That mouse has no sense at all and no manners either. Takes after his father.'

'Not one of yours, then?'

'No, definitely not. My young are well brought up. Slickwhiskers and me, we're very strict.'

'Consider it done,' said Hannibal. 'In fairness, though, I think you ought to warn him. Besides, it's no fun for me if I've only got to stick out a paw. I like a chase.' His eyes gleamed and for a moment he was the lean, deadly killer that Scratchbelly had first known.

'I'll speak to Nutcruncher. Not that it'll do much good,' he said. 'Now let's change the subject. Any news?'

'Lots of it, and not good,' said the cat. There was a pause as he bit suddenly into the fur of his front leg. 'Dogging fleas! And talking of dogs – that's what the Humans are doing. Talking about getting one.'

'You understand them, then?' said Scratchbelly. 'All I hear is so loud you can't make any sense of it.'

'Yes, it is loud. Best to listen from two rooms away. I don't follow most of it,' admitted Hannibal. 'A lot of it is pretty boring anyway; always on about somewhere called Werk, things like that. But they're definitely going to get a dog. The Male wants one.'

'Bad news for you.'

'For both of us,' said the cat.

'Not for us mice, surely?' said Scratchbelly. 'I was told dogs aren't much good at mousing.'

'Depends on the dog,' said Hannibal. 'The

farm terriers would kill anything – mice, rats, cats, you name it. When it came to rats, they were better than us, even. But the bigger dogs – well, you could be right. They're inclined to fall over their own feet when they try for a mouse. But all dogs have one thing in common that'll cause you problems. They smell.'

'Well, I daresay they do,' said Scratchbelly after a puzzled pause. 'But that's not exactly a problem, surely? I mean, I'm sure we'll get used to it, however bad it is—'

'No,' said Hannibal patiently, 'I mean, they can smell. That is, they can use their noses. Pick up scents. You follow? Their noses are brilliant – certainly better than mine, and probably yours too.'

'OK. They can smell us,' said Scratchbelly. 'So what? So long as they can't get at us, it doesn't matter.'

Hannibal sighed. 'Oh, but it does,' he said quietly. 'You see, dogs have something else in common. They have no self-respect.'

'What do you mean?'

'It's a bit difficult to explain. Take me,' said Hannibal. 'I live in this house with the Humans. They call me Their Cat and think I'm there to keep down – well, you; and that I do it for them. All rubbish of course. If they weren't feeding me to bursting I would catch mice all right, but it would be for me, not them: it's just natural to me. Of course I rub round them a bit sometimes but that's just to keep the grub coming. Now dogs, dogs are different. They actually like Humans and want to be useful to them: they're never happier than when they're enslaving themselves.' He curled his lip contemptuously. 'There was a sheepdog at the farm – spent all his life chasing sheep for the farmer and never ate a single one. Incredible. And he was so proud of himself – always on about his Duty to his Master. I'll say this for the terriers, they never came out with such nonsense. Oh, and then there was the Labrador: even worse. Went everywhere with the farmer – guarding him, he said – and when the farmer shot something he'd bring it back in his mouth and hand it over. Amazing. Give *me* the chance to wrap myself round a pheasant, you wouldn't see me for two days.'

'All right, so dogs are slaves to Humans,' said Scratchbelly. 'I still don't see—'

'Look,' said Hannibal. 'If I chase a mouse into a hole what happens?'

'You wait outside for a bit and then go away.'

'Correct. But I wait quietly. The Humans don't know why I'm there. They probably think I'm dozing. Whereas a dog will smell your mouse-holes and will tell the Humans about them, and go on telling them. Humans are pretty stupid but eventually they'll get the message. And then they will Do Something about you.'

Scratchbelly frowned. 'Yes, I see that could be a problem. Still, let's hope for the best. Perhaps they'll forget about getting one. After all, they've other things to think about. The Female is nearly due to give birth, isn't she?

How many, do you reckon?'

'No idea,' said Hannibal. 'About five, by the size of her.'

Scratchbelly nodded. 'Well, I'd better go and see Nutcruncher about his Number Seven.'

'Seven seems a lot,' said Hannibal. 'How many's he got?'

'Would you believe, fifteen. Three litters. Six almost full-grown.' Scratchbelly sniffed. 'He goes in for quantity rather than quality.'

The interview with Nutcruncher did not go well.

Nutcruncher was the son of Scratchbelly's brother Flashfoot, who had met his end in a trap. Nutcruncher, therefore, was younger and larger than his uncle, but, Scratchbelly thought, he lacked the intelligence needed in a good clan leader.

Scratchbelly found his nephew in the Nutcruncher chamber, which was handily sited in the wall dividing the kitchen from the utility room.

'You'll have to do something about your Number Seven,' he said without preamble. 'Hannibal's had enough of his stupidity and his manners. He's called off the truce, at least as far as Seven is concerned. I'm not surprised. That mouse's behaviour is appalling.'

Nutcruncher was, for a mouse, distinctly square-jawed: it gave him a stubborn, morose expression which, as it happened, suited his personality.

'Nothing wrong with my Number Seven,' he said pugnaciously. 'Nothing wrong with a few high spirits in a youngster. And anyway, who are you to tell me how to go on? I'm a clan leader, same as you. Of course, I'm not the Cat's Friend, like you.'

Scratchbelly felt his temper rising. 'Look,' he said sharply. 'If it wasn't for me, your life would be a lot less peaceful – if you had much of a life left, that is, which, given your brain-power, is unlikely. Anyway, I've told you the situation: the rest is up to you. Now I must get back to my family.' He turned to go.

'Oh yes,' said Nutcruncher spitefully. 'To your *little* family.'

Scratchbelly stopped in mid-turn. 'What do you mean by that?'

Nutcruncher grinned unpleasantly. 'How many has Slickwhiskers had, the last lot? Six, wasn't it? No wonder your young are well-behaved, you've got so few to worry about. Now with my *fifteen*, it's not so easy. They're nearly full-grown, ready to be given names. I've been thinking—'

'Makes a change,' said Scratchbelly sarcastically.

'Seems to me that a family my size needs more room. Our territory is about the same but there's fewer of you. Seems to me we should have more, especially round the kitchen. I've got a lot of mouths to feed.'

'I'll think about it,' said Scratchbelly carefully. He didn't want a feud unless it was absolutely necessary.

He returned to his own main chamber.

Slickwhiskers was there with her six new young and Old Grey, his ancient and arthritic sire who had voluntarily yielded to him the title of Chief Mouse.

'Trouble?' said Old Grey; his bones creaked and his hearing was going but Old Grey's instincts remained razor-sharp.

'Possibly,' said Scratchbelly, and told them of his meetings with Hannibal and Nutcruncher. While he was speaking two of his three older offspring, Sidestepper and Flickerear, came into the chamber.

'I'm not surprised at Nutcruncher's attitude,' said Sidestepper. 'His lot have been giving all four of us plenty of stick lately. Mostly verbal, but I nearly had to fight his Number Four.'

'Well, there'll probably be one less soon,' said Scratchbelly, 'unless Hannibal has slowed up.'

'Mind you keep out of his way, you two,' said Slickwhiskers. 'A cat going after a mouse doesn't always have time to check on who he's chasing.'

2

The next day began well for the Scratchbellys when the Male Human decided to enliven his morning muesli with some dried fruit and, opening the bag with too much haste and energy, sent a significant proportion of its contents over the back of the kitchen units. The fruit fell just outside one of Scratchbelly's holes, and they were able to feast effortlessly.

But after that things deteriorated rapidly.

Scratchbelly was lying back comfortably with

a full tummy when Nutcruncher suddenly burst into the chamber. He was clearly very angry.

'Your poisonous cat! He's had my Number Seven. So much for your cat-dealing. I thought you were supposed to have him under control. My guess is, you have. One rule for the Scratchbellys, another for Nutcrunchers, is that it? Trying to even up the numbers—'

'That's enough!' said Scratchbelly sharply. 'I warned you about Number Seven. You obviously didn't pass it on – that's down to you. Let me tell you, we're lucky Hannibal didn't declare open season on the lot of us. I don't control him, as you put it. I don't like your tone and I don't like your manners, bursting in here like that. So now, please go.'

'Going!' snarled Nutcruncher as he turned back into a run. 'This isn't the end of it, Scratchbelly. I meant what I said about needing more territory. Now I'm going to do something about it.'

Scratchbelly waited until he had

disappeared, then left the chamber and made his way to the hole in the fireplace. There was no sign of Hannibal or of the Humans. Scratchbelly decided to risk a shout. He was fairly sure that no Human outside the room would hear him.

'Hannibal!' he roared. Nothing happened for about a minute. Then the sitting-room door opened slightly and the black cat stalked across to the fireplace rug, sat and began to wash.

'You didn't waste any time,' said Scratchbelly. 'Not that I'm complaining,' he added hurriedly. 'I'm glad to see the last of the silly little fool.'

'Can't say I blame you,' said Hannibal. 'I tell you, if I hadn't been there the Humans would have seen him for certain. He was running down the middle of the hall in broad daylight. Ridiculous. I went after him and blow me if he didn't turn round and try to run straight underneath me.' He shook his head in wonder. 'I had to think fast – never happened to me before. In the end I just did a little jump and brought all four feet down on him, claws out. Most unstylish. I'm glad no one saw.'

'I trust you ate him all up?' said Scratchbelly anxiously. 'I wouldn't like the Humans to find any sign of us.'

'Yeah, I ate him.' Hannibal made a face. 'That wasn't much fun either. That mouse was full of – well I don't know what it was, but it smelt horrible and tasted worse.'

'Garlic,' said Scratchbelly. 'All the Nutcrunchers reek of it. The spice cupboard is in their territory.'

'Well, I don't like it,' said the cat. 'Now, hot news. The humans have got a dog. Arrived about an hour ago.'

'Oh dear. What's he like?'

'Big. Full-grown. I was hoping for a puppy. You can put a puppy in his place for keeps. Of course he tried it on,' said Hannibal contemptuously. 'Came snorting up to me, saying, 'Get going, Sooty' – stuff like that.

I patted him on the nose to warn him but he kept on so I gave him a sharp one, claws out. That fixed him for the time being. He tells me he's a red setter – a gundog, like a Labrador. That means he's got a superb nose: if an ant broke wind, he'd know about it. Bad news for you.'

'Where is he now, then?'

'The Male Human took him for a walk as far as I can gather.' Hannibal shook his head again. 'Or perhaps it was the other way round. I don't understand it. It didn't happen at the farm.' He jerked his head round suddenly: both of them had heard the front door opening. 'Looks like you're going to get a sight of him.'

He had hardly finished speaking when the door swung open and the dog bounded over to the fireplace. Hannibal pointedly turned his back. Scratchbelly had an indistinct impression of an immensely high mass of reddish-brown hair, huge feet, massive teeth framing an equally massive tongue and an enormous, glistening nose which was coming straight at him. He backed swiftly into safety, then quivered in a tremendous blast of sound as the dog started shouting.

'Mouse! Mouse! Here, quick! Come on! Come on!' roared the dog. Hannibal slunk off unhurriedly as the Male Human came in and grabbed the dog, saying something which Scratchbelly could not decipher. The dog, still shouting, was dragged away.

Scratchbelly returned to the chamber. By a lucky chance all the family were there or nearby and he was able to call them together quickly.

'A dog's arrived,' he said. 'Keep out of his way, obviously; but the worst is, he's got a fantastic nose and will certainly tell the Humans about most or all of our holes. We can't do much about that, but be on the lookout for traps and poison when they get the message.'

'What about Hannibal?' said Sidestepper. 'If

the Humans know we're here, they'll expect him to be doing something about it.'

Scratchbelly looked at him. 'True,' he said slowly. 'Sidestepper – a job for you. I want you to bring us as many garlic cloves as you can.'

'I'll need help,' said Sidestepper. 'The spice cupboard is Nutcruncher territory. They're not going to let us go there.'

'Take whoever you want,' said Scratchbelly.

'I'll take Flickerear, please,' said Sidestepper. 'OK with you, sis?'

'Sure,' said Flickerear. She continued meticulously cleaning her whiskers. 'Ready when you are.'

'Very well,' said Scratchbelly. 'It's time for the rest of us to be out foraging – so let's get to it.'

Scratchbelly decided to give the kitchen a wide berth and, after a moment's cogitation, slipped quietly out of the hole in the outside wall into the garden. After his journey of a few weeks before the Open no longer filled him with terror and he had made several brief visits to it. He still preferred the house and didn't go far from it, staying close to the house path and border and never venturing on to the lawn. He was cautiously and slowly adapting to the feeling of exposure, which had initially troubled him severely. And there was an abundant supply of food out there, which was a big plus. This evening he quickly came across a neat line of lightly covered nasturtium seeds: he gobbled greedily and, when he was comfortably full, stuffed four of them into his cheeks, slipped back into the wall and returned unhurriedly to the family chamber. Slickwhiskers, after a brief foray into the dining-room, had returned early with her young; he dropped the seeds close to her and they touched noses. Then an unaccustomed scraping sound in the passage made them both turn rapidly. It materialized as a large garlic clove slowly entering the chamber. Sidestepper's head appeared round the side of it.

'We've cleared them out of garlic,' he said cheerfully. 'There were only two cloves left. Flickerear is bringing the other one.' As he spoke, it appeared in the entrance and Flickerear pushed it into a corner. Both mice were panting from their exertions.

'How did it go?' asked Scratchbelly.

'Pretty well,' said Sidestepper. 'We spotted four of the Nutcrunchers in the kitchen near the spice cupboard so I sent Flickerear to distract them while I slipped round and got in.'

'How did she distract them?' asked Scratchbelly but Slickwhiskers was ahead of him.

'Flickerear!' she said sharply. 'I hope you weren't too forward!'

Flickerear looked up from polishing her coat. 'Oh, Mother,' she sighed heavily. 'I had to distract them, didn't I? Of course I was forward.'

'Anyway,' Sidestepper hurried on to forestall the maternal outburst which was clearly coming, 'I rolled the cloves out of the door and dropped them behind the cooker; then got down without them seeing and pushed them along the wall to the hole by the sink. When Flickerear came back we pushed them along to here, hoping we didn't bump into any Nutcrunchers – and we didn't.'

'How did you get away from them?' said Slickwhiskers to Flickerear.

'No problem,' said her daughter airily. 'They were very young and not too bright. I just used Scorn.'

While they were speaking, Tailtwist, Sidestepper's and Flickerear's brother, came in. Slickwhiskers gave a wail. He was limping badly and blood was pouring from a tear in his ear.

'Had a bit of trouble,' he said huskily. 'Ran into three Nutcrunchers in the kitchen – *our* part of it, mind you – and they threw me out. I got a good bite into one of them but I had to give ground in the end. They said the kitchen's theirs now and we're to keep out.'

'Never mind,' said Scratchbelly, as Slickwhiskers began licking Tailtwist's ravaged ear. 'You did your best.'

'And it wasn't wasted,' said Sidestepper. 'It was probably because of you that we got the garlic back without trouble.'

'Ah yes, the garlic,' said Scratchbelly. 'Now, all of you, get stuck into it. I want you all reeking of it. There's enough here to last us for a good while.'

There was a chorus of dissenting groans.

'I'm not eating it,' said Old Grey firmly. 'Garlic gives me wind.'

'Old Grey, everything gives you wind.'

Old Grey grunted. Slickwhiskers turned to her mate. 'Do the little ones have to eat it as well?'

'They've been going out. I want everyone who goes out to have it. It's a precaution.'

There were more groans and pulled faces, but Scratchbelly's authority was unquestioned and the chamber soon echoed to the sound of reluctant munching.

3

The next two days were difficult. The dog was, as Hannibal had predicted, quick to locate their holes and bellowed the information regularly to the Humans. It was not difficult to avoid him when out foraging for he took no pains to conceal his movements. Sidestepper, who was inclined to take risks, was seen by him on one occasion. The dog gave inexpert chase and shouted even louder than before; but the Humans were preoccupied and even less observant than usual.

The kitchen was closed to the Scratchbellys: all entrances were patrolled by at least three Nutcrunchers. After some hesitation, Scratchbelly ordered a foraging expedition outside the house. It went very well. He was pleased to see that his younger offspring conducted themselves sensibly and seemed to adapt well to the Open. They returned well-filled with a variety of flower seeds.

'That was good. Maybe we should just move out,' said Slickwhiskers. Scratchbelly shook his head. Life in the house was comfortable and relatively predictable. Besides, he didn't want to surrender meekly to Nutcruncher.

Shortly after their return, they all heard an unusual sound: the cat was calling, loudly enough to be heard in the chamber. 'Scratchbelly! Scratchbelly! Where are you? Meet me. Urgent!'

Scratchbelly hurried to the fireplace with a

heavy heart. He knew what was coming.

'The Humans have woken up at last,' said Hannibal. 'The dog found a hole in the utility room – the one by the freezer – and was trying to stick his nose into it when the Female walked in. You can expect trouble now.'

'I was expecting it sooner or later.'

'I'm afraid I'll have to be part of it. They're accusing me of not doing my job.'

'Well, you haven't been.'

'True. But they'll cut off the Kittymeat and make me catch my own dinner. I can't put up with that. I'm fat and intend to stay that way. So I'll have to give them some bodies to look at.' He snarled irritably. 'Even then I'll be on short commons. It's all the fault of that dogging . . . er . . . dog. They were neglecting me even before he put them on to you. And as long as he's around he'll be showing them your holes and I'll be expected to come up with the goods.'

'You keep saying "he". Doesn't this dog have a name?'

'Yes, a really fine one. They've called him Seizer,' said the cat discontentedly. 'How they could give him a good name like that and me a dumb one like Hannibal I'll never know.'

'Yes. Well, thanks for the warning,' said Scratchbelly sadly. 'Look – I realize your position, and of course we'll all be at risk. But if you concentrated on the kitchen and the utility room, you'd be doing me a favour.' And he explained the Nutcruncher problem.

'Hmm,' said the cat. 'Trouble is, aren't they the garlic ones? All right for laying on the fireplace but not much good for eating.'

'No. We're the garlic ones now.'

'I thought I could smell it. You crafty devil.' Hannibal gave a short chuckle. 'I'll do as you ask. Be seeing you.'

'Not if I see you first, from now on.'

'No,' said the cat, sounding almost sad. 'I suppose you're right.'

4

Scratchbelly returned to the family chamber to deliver the unwelcome news. The new youngsters – Numbers One to Six – were told of Hannibal's deadly speed and accuracy in bloodcurdling detail: both Scratchbelly and Slickwhiskers set much store by the old mouse saying, 'A mouse without Fear will not long be Here.'

'I suppose I must warn Nutcruncher, even if we are at war with him,' said Scratchbelly.

'We're all mice after all. You come with me, Slickwhiskers, to show that we want to parley.'

Nutcruncher was his usual graceless self. 'Clear off, you,' he said rudely. 'You're not welcome on our territory. I thought my lot had made that clear.'

'It would have been nice if you'd had the decency to make it clear yourself,' said Scratchbelly icily. 'Your attack on Tailtwist was a disgusting breach of etiquette. You should have stated your territorial claim first.'

'I did.'

'No. Bombast and threats, but no formal declaration. I hardly know why I've taken the trouble to come here at all, but the fact is I'm here to warn you that the dog has alerted the Humans to our presence – or, to be precise, to yours, as he showed them one of your holes. As a result, Hannibal has been forced to return to mousing. We can also expect the usual traps, poison and hole-blocking.'

'Huh. So much for making deals with cats.'

Scratchbelly fought down his rising temper. 'That's all I came to say. We'll be on our way.'

'Good riddance,' said Nutcruncher. 'Oh, by the way, are you getting used to the Open? You'll need to.' He chuckled unpleasantly.

The mice grimly awaited the appearance of traps and poison; but none came. In the very early hours of the following morning – at a time when they could normally rely on Human inactivity – there was a sudden flashing-on of lights and banging of doors. The foraging mice were taken wholly by surprise. There was a frantic rush to the holes or any other form of shelter and many panic-stricken shouts of 'Get out of the way!' Scratchbelly took temporary refuge under the dining-room china cabinet. A moment later Hannibal came in, yawning and ill-tempered.

'Hannibal! What's happening?'

'I've been kicked out of the airing cupboard, that's what,' said Hannibal, carefully avoiding looking towards the cabinet. 'It seems the

Female Human is about to give birth. They're both going off in the car.'

'What for?'

'How should I know? Perhaps she prefers to have her young there. Look out.' He turned towards the door. 'Here comes Seizer.'

The dog loped in. 'Ah, there you are, cat. The Master has left me on guard,' he said importantly. 'You are, I suppose, on pest control? If not, you should be. If you see or hear anything suspicious coming from outside let me know immediately. I shall be on duty by the front door.'

The cat gave him a long wordless look, then rose and settled himself elaborately and comfortably on the dining-room table. The dog started to speak, changed his mind and went out. Scratchbelly allowed a decent interval to elapse before slipping out from under the cabinet to return home.

The Male Human came back alone next day. A few days later the Female returned with her

young. In the interim traps and poison – but, surprisingly, no hole-blocking – at last made their appearance. The Scratchbellys were vigilant and thankfully none of the family was lost. Sidestepper, who had taken to surreptitiously visiting the kitchen area and listening to the Nutcrunchers' conversations, reported that Nutcruncher Number Three had died in a trap in the utility room and that there was much vituperation directed at Hannibal, but for what reason he couldn't discover. Seizer meanwhile continued to nose into holes and shout 'Mouse!' at frequent intervals.

Scratchbelly visited the fireplace from time to time in the hope of a safe conversation with Hannibal. After several unsuccessful attempts his hope was realized.

'I gather you've been causing problems in the kitchen,' said Scratchbelly.

'Got two of them. Different nights. I waited on the kitchen table for the first – a good quick leap,' said the cat, grinning. 'The second was a straight floor-chase, quite easy. He was very slow to spot me. I don't think these Nutcrunchers are too bright.'

'I suppose you showed them to the Humans?'

Hannibal made a wry face. 'I put the first one on the fireplace tiles and you know what happened? That – that dog came in and sniffed round it and called the Humans, and they thought he'd caught it. Seizer! He couldn't catch a mouse if it stood on his tongue. And the Humans are saying, "Good boy" and "Well, Hannibal, isn't he clever?" and suchlike rubbish. So in the end I ate that mouse and the other one. Still a bit garlicky, but not too bad. But I tell you: that dog's got to go.'

'What's happened to the Human young?' asked Scratchbelly. 'We've not seen a sign of them.'

'You mean It,' said the cat. 'There's only one of 'em. Pathetic. Mind you, it's absolutely huge. They keep it upstairs in the spare room, in a sort of cage. I haven't seen much of it either because Seizer has decided it's his duty to guard it for his beloved Masters. He even sleeps under the cage now, instead of in their room. Still, at least it keeps him out of my whiskers.'

'You mean he's there all night?'

'Yes. And a lot of the day too.'

Scratchbelly was silent for a moment, concentrating on the beginning of an idea.

Then he said, 'I must be going. Keep up the good work in the kitchen.'

'Oh, I will,' said the cat. 'It looks like the only way to get any grub.'

5

Back in the chamber Scratchbelly found Sidestepper talking to Old Grey. The younger mouse was holding a large piece of biscuit and looking very pleased with himself.

'Your boy,' said Old Grey severely, 'has been taking chances again.'

'Where've you been now?' said Scratchbelly resignedly.

'In the kitchen. Yes, I know you said not to, but Hannibal's been making his presence felt there and it gave me an idea. All the wall-runs to the kitchen are guarded by Nutcrunchers of course, but they can't guard the kitchen door; and I'd noticed it was open. Hannibal was safely in the sitting-room – it looked as if he was talking to you – so I went to our dining-room hole and dashed out of it across the floor and through into the kitchen shouting, 'Look out! Cat! Cat! Run!' The Nutcrunchers who were out foraging didn't stop to ask questions, just dropped everything and went for the holes. I grabbed this biscuit and went with them and was away down the run before they got their brains into gear.'

'Didn't they come after you?'

'Oh yes, three of them. They came into our territory. But Tailtwist came in from the Open just after I passed the outside hole and they ran right into him. He really tore into them, Dad. Of course I went back to help but to be honest I didn't have to do much. They soon turned and ran. You should see the run: blood

everywhere, and all of it Nutcrunchers'!
Tailtwist was terrific.'

His brother, who had come in during
Sidestepper's story, went pink in the ears. 'I
caught them by surprise,' he said modestly.

'You've both done very well,' said
Scratchbelly warmly. 'Er . . . Sidestepper. A
word.'

Tailtwist tactfully took a piece of biscuit and
went out.

'Hannibal says, and I agree, that Seizer the
dog has got to go,' said Scratchbelly. He briefly
told Sidestepper what he had learned from the
cat.

'The dog is with the Human young all night.
That set me thinking. You remember when the
Female went off to give birth? I don't know
about you, but I got the feeling that both the
Humans, especially the Male, were very
irritable; and it occurs to me that they don't
like being woken up during the night. Even
though they sleep an appalling amount.'

'You're right.' Old Grey's voice came in unexpectedly. 'My father knocked a bottle off the kitchen shelf at night-time once. The crash woke the Humans living here then, and they all came down the stairs, furious. Shouted at each other, my father said. 'Course, he was back in the hole when they arrived.'

'Good,' said Scratchbelly. 'My idea is this. We get into the room where the young's cage is after they're asleep. Seizer will be there as usual. Now, when he spots us, what will he do?'

'He'll shout to them about us.' Sidestepper grinned suddenly. 'He'll shout until they come. And they won't be happy.'

'Right. We disappear, of course, as soon as we've got him going. And then come back later and set him off again. They might even think he's attacking their young, with luck. If we can keep him roaring, they're bound to get rid of him.'

'It's a great idea, Dad,' said Sidestepper. He frowned suddenly. 'Just one problem. How do we get into the young's room? There are very few runs in the walls upstairs and I don't think there are any in the young's room. We can go up the stairs – risky, but we can.'

'That's right,' said Old Grey, 'but if the door is closed, you can't go under it. Too tight. Unless they've changed the door since I was last up there.'

Scratchbelly looked at Sidestepper. They both shook their heads. To gamble on an open door was foolhardy. Sidestepper murmured the old mouse dictum, 'The Wise expect the Worst.'

'Good lad,' said Old Grey, who had taught it to him.

There was a doleful silence for a moment. Then suddenly Scratchbelly gave a yell.

'The creeper!'

Sidestepper grinned. 'Yes, the Virginia creeper! It goes right up to the window!' His grin disappeared. 'So long as the window's open.'

But Scratchbelly was not to be discouraged. 'They always leave windows open; look at the kitchen, the dining-room. I think they like to be cold. I bet they leave the upstairs ones open too.' He sobered slightly. 'We'll have to check it first.'

'I'm on my way,' said Sidestepper.

When Sidestepper had gone, Scratchbelly also left the chamber and made a somewhat unsuccessful attempt at foraging in the dining-room. He was returning with a sliver of lettuce when he heard noises in the sitting-room and quickened his step, knowing that Hannibal was capable of appearing with terrible suddenness; but his fears proved unwarranted.

Slickwhiskers met him in the run. 'We've lost one of the young ones,' she said curtly. 'Number Two. He slipped and fell out of the fireplace hole, straight on to the rug. Hannibal was lying on it, so that was that.' She gave no sign of her real feelings, but Scratchbelly sensed her sorrow.

'We must expect to lose some,' he said quietly. It was supposed to sound comforting. 'You know, we always lose one or two.'

'Numbers are more important now, with this Nutcruncher feud.'

'True. We can't do much about that, I'm afraid, but at least they're losing more than us. And I'm working on something which might, eventually, get Hannibal off our backs.'

'What?' she said. But he wouldn't tell her. Slickwhiskers didn't like risks; and in any case, until Sidestepper got back, everything was only speculation.

Sidestepper returned at last, tired but elated. 'The window is open all right. Just wide enough. And the climb up the creeper is easy, with quite a lot of old leaves to give some cover. It's a bit exposed in places, but should be fine in the dark. And I don't think a bird could take you off there – it's too close to the wall.'

Sidestepper had never seen an owl, or he might have been less confident. 'It takes a while to get to the window-sill, though, and it's quite a jump from creeper to sill.'

'Did you try it?'

'Oh yes. Not really difficult. Might be tricky in a wind.'

'Good,' said Scratchbelly. 'Well, no point in waiting. We'll go tonight.'

6

They did not start out until Scratchbelly felt sure that midnight had long passed. The creeper fortunately grew next to the wall-side path so that by keeping to the border they were able to get to it with minimum exposure to the Open. The creeper itself provided excellent protection during the climb. It was well-established and its tendrils crossed and recrossed each other, making a good, thick layer, so that for much of the time the mice were totally concealed.

'You weren't joking about it taking a while,' said Scratchbelly. He was finding the climb hard going.

'Not much further,' said Sidestepper; and, soon after, 'I'm level with the sill. Now we jump.'

The creeper had been cut away beneath the window but allowed to grow up the side of it, so the leap was more or less horizontal and not physically demanding. It was, however, nerve-racking at that immense height, and the window-sill had an uncomfortably polished, slippery look. Sidestepper, making the manoeuvre for a second time, went over without trouble, but Scratchbelly slewed badly on landing, slid headfirst towards the darkness and was only saved by Sidestepper, who sank his teeth into his father's tail and clung determinedly to the sill.

'Ouch! Thanks,' said Scratchbelly as he eased himself backwards. The two mice gazed for a moment over the moonlit garden. Sidestepper drew in his breath.

'It's marvellous up here,' he said. 'I'm going to come here more often.'

Scratchbelly said nothing, but jerked his head to the left. The owl passed just below them on silent wings, its head lowered to scan the lawn: it slowed a little, then turned away, steadily losing height as it flew parallel with the next-door hedge, lifted over it and was gone.

'Not too often, if you know what's good for you,' said Scratchbelly. 'Mind you, he'd hardly expect us to be up here. But I'll be happier when we're through the window and back inside.'

The window was still open. They looked in to plan their next move.

'The young's cage is right beneath the inside sill,' said Scratchbelly. 'Can't see Seizer, though.'

Sidestepper ran to the other end of the sill and back again.

'He's underneath the cage. I could see his tail sticking out.'

'The sill's not far from the floor,' said Scratchbelly. 'Seizer could reach us there, and

the Humans would probably see us. We'll go
for the shelves.'

Sidestepper nodded. 'Up the curtain, along
the rail and – another jump,' he said. 'You
won't fall off, will you Dad?'

Scratchbelly gave him a look and led the way in. The room was surprisingly noisy, for both the Human young and the dog were snoring. The dog was much the loudest, his snores interspersed with soft little whines. The two mice reached the shelving without trouble and looked down from a safe height, well hidden by jars, small bottles and a few books. The other two occupants of the room snored on.

'Some guardian,' said Scratchbelly contemptuously. 'This is no good. We'll have to wake him up.'

He stepped forward to the shelf edge and shouted at the top of his voice. 'Oi! You! Seizer! Stink-breath! Open your loppy lugs you dozy doormat!'

Sidestepper joined in lustily. For a while nothing happened. The mice were getting hoarse when Seizer at last awoke.

The transition from sleep to wakefulness was impressively rapid. Scratchbelly retreated involuntarily to the back of his comfortably out-of-reach shelf as Seizer leapt up, scrabbling high on the wall with his front feet as he roared, 'Mouse! Mice! Come quick!' at the top of his voice. The Human young woke and added a thin, ineffectual wailing to the commotion.

The expected response was quick to follow. There was a loud bang from a nearby door. Immediately the mice leapt for the curtain rail, dropped to the sill and were outside looking in when a light flashed on and the Human Male appeared. His hair was dishevelled, hanging over half-closed eyes. The mice listened contentedly to his bellowing, which was as usual incomprehensible but was obviously a strong rebuke to Seizer. The dog cowered but still tried to get his message through.

'Sorry, sorry but – mice! Mice! On the shelf! Oh Master, so sorry, so sorry. Gone now, but mice were – really very, very sorry . . .'

'Talk about dogged determination,' said Sidestepper, grinning.

A really enormous roar from the Human at

last silenced Seizer. The young continued to wail weakly for a few minutes and then fell silent. The room was plunged into darkness as the Male left. Seizer paced mutely and exasperatedly back and forth in the darkness, chastened but not, apparently, totally disgraced.

'Nearly but not quite,' said Scratchbelly disappointedly. 'Oh well, we'll just have to go back in again. Let the Human settle down first, though.'

The wind had risen and a light, cold rain began to fall. The moon disappeared and the two mice looked disconsolately out into deep blackness, broken only by distant orange-coloured street lights. Sidestepper wondered what they were.

'Human stuff. Not our concern,' said Scratchbelly, hoping in vain to conceal his ignorance. 'This is pretty miserable; but we mustn't go in too soon. I suggest you recite the Survival Laws to pass the time.'

Sidestepper as an adult, named mouse was

technically no longer subject to this sort of thing, but he complied without demur. 'Use ears and nose before eyes, for eyes can be seen . . .' he began. The long litany went on and on: Scratchbelly nodded from time to time and prompted occasionally. At last Sidestepper fell silent.

'Very good,' said Scratchbelly. 'Well, I think we could try again now.'

Seizer had returned to his place under the cage but this time was only half asleep. By the time they had reached the shelf he was in full cry, shouting and leaping towards them energetically.

'He almost got a paw on to the shelf then,' said Scratchbelly conversationally to his offspring. 'Look – if I shove this bottle over, the Humans will think it was him. With luck, that'll do for him for sure.'

It was a very small bottle containing a few pills, but it stuck at his first attempt. He heard the Humans approaching and made a hurried, determined charge at it. The bottle this time made little resistance, far less than he expected. As it fell he realized to his horror that he had overdone it: unable to control his impetus, he flew off the shelf and fell towards the panting dog.

Scratchbelly's world went momentarily even darker than before. Mentally resigned to his death even as he fell, he thought at first that he was in Seizer's mouth. Then came a blinding glare. He looked upward in confusion. All he could see was a round patch of blazing light a short distance above him; all round him was a circular wall, sheer and patently unclimbable. He shared his limited space with some cloths, a bottle and a large tin.

He had scarcely registered these facts when Seizer's huge muzzle appeared above him, the teeth much in evidence. The dog was still shouting, telling the Humans of his presence and clearly hoping to prove it by producing

Scratchbelly for inspection. Scratchbelly was about to bury himself hopelessly under the cloths when the dog's great head suddenly disappeared with a jerk, accompanied by a tremendous roar from both the Humans.

Instinctively, Scratchbelly still buried himself under the cloths. He heard a great deal of noise from the dog, the two adult Humans and their young; it made his senses whirl and he cowered, terrified, unthinking and immobile.

Abruptly the noises receded and darkness returned. There was total silence for about a minute. It was broken by Sidestepper's voice from far above.

'Dad! Are you all right?'

'I think so. Where am I?'

'You fell into a bucket. Seizer took a moment to work out where you were and the Humans grabbed him and shouted at him. Really angry, they were. I think it's worked, Dad. He kept on telling them where you were and they just dragged him out. They took their young as well; it was howling and wouldn't stop.'

'Good. But Sidestepper, I can't get out of here.'

'I'll come down and see what I can do.'

But it was no good. The bucket was too heavy for Sidestepper to push over. He tried sitting on the edge and trailing his tail while Scratchbelly climbed on to the tin and leapt upward to catch it; but the gap was too great.

'Any other ideas?' said Scratchbelly dispiritedly.

Sidestepper shook his head. 'I'll have to fetch the others. Perhaps, if we hung on to each other's tails—' he broke off at the sound of Human footsteps. 'They're coming back!'

Sidestepper disappeared. The Human came in very quietly – for a Human – and did not switch on the light. Scratchbelly, sightless in his bucket, was nevertheless able to identify it as the Female by the gentle muttering which she made to her young, whom she had clearly brought with her. There was a rattling from the cage and sundry other noises; after a short interval, the female left, closing the door. The rhythmic sound of the young's breathing rose and fell in the darkness. Then came another sound, familiar and unexpected.

'Dad! Are you there?'

'Of course I'm here,' said Scratchbelly testily. 'Where else? And what are you still here for? I thought you'd be halfway down the wall by now, to get help.'

'Um . . . bit of a mess-up I'm afraid. When the Human came in I went up the side of the cage to get to the window – it's the quickest route from here – but I slipped and fell in. There's lots of soft stuff – blankets – in it and I got a bit tangled up, and the Human came straight over so I didn't dare to jump out through the side. So I burrowed down into it while she put her young in. She nearly put it right on top of me, and I had to move smartish. Ended up by the young's feet – up against one of them in fact.'

'You're lucky it didn't wake up.'

'Yes. It did twitch a bit. When the Human had gone, I came out very carefully.'

'All right,' said Scratchbelly. 'Now, don't waste any more time. Get through that window and bring some help up here.'

'Um . . . There's a bit more. She shut the window.'

There was a moment's silence.

'So,' said Scratchbelly at length. 'You can't get out until the Humans come back.'

'No.'

'And I can't get out at all.'

'No.'

'There's only one thing to do then.'

'Yes.'

So they both went to sleep.

7

Scratchbelly's was a rude awakening. Roused by the sound of Human footsteps, he just had time to register that the room was full of early morning light and that he was very hungry before he was thrown on his side as the bucket jerked upwards. He scrambled to his feet and buried himself in the cloths as the bucket, swinging steadily, moved through the air. Glancing up he could see the handle and the huge Human hand gripping it. The bucket stopped its forward movement briefly and, from the sounds above, Scratchbelly gathered that the Human had picked up her young from the cage. Then the bucket lurched and moved on again. Gazing at the ceiling, Scratchbelly realized that they had left the room and, as the bucket embarked on a series of disconcerting downward jerks, that they were descending the stairs. He hoped, fleetingly, that Sidestepper had managed to escape through the door. At last the bucket struck solid floor with a jarring that almost brought the tin over on top of him. The hand disappeared.

Scratchbelly tensed himself, half expecting discovery in the next few seconds. It didn't happen. He heard the Human move away but sensed that she had not moved far and then he heard both of the Human voices, deafening as always. He raised his nose, sniffed and identified his surroundings. He was in the dining-room, only metres from his entrance hole under the china cabinet. From the centre of the room came a tantalizing smell of cereals – the big flakes of corn which featured prominently in his diet. His hunger returned in force, and he decided to investigate the contents of the tin. He scrambled to the top of it; the lid was fastened tight, but there was a white, flour-like powder round it which he licked tentatively. Both taste and smell were unpleasant and he quickly decided that the food value was nil.

'Hello, hello,' said a familiar voice above him. 'What have we here?'

Scratchbelly looked up into Hannibal's big, yellow eyes.

'Ah . . . good morning. Looks like my luck's run out,' he said resignedly. 'Well, no complaints. Get on with it.'

'Hang on a minute,' said Hannibal. 'Seems to me I owe you a favour. I don't know what you've been up to upstairs but you've got rid of Seizer; he's been shut out in the garden shed, still shouting about mice. And I've had a good night: got three in the kitchen. The Male Human saw me catch one, so I'm right back in their good books. He came down in the middle of the night – that was to do with you, too – and switched on the light just as I pounced. It wasn't exactly a difficult kill, mind. Those kitchen mice are pretty hopeless. The one he saw actually came out from under the cooker backwards. Unforgivable.' He glanced briefly over his shoulder. 'The Humans are eating at the table. Female's holding her young. I think we'd better put on a show for them.'

'Anything you say, Hannibal. And . . . thank you.'

'Right. Listen carefully. I'm going to push the bucket over. I'll try to make it fall towards the door to the hall. Go flat out towards it. You'll have to go close to the Humans but so long as you move fast you'll be all right. You know how slow they are. Now, when you get to the doorway there's a little mat-rug thing, you know the one?'

'Yes. It's got a sort of flower on it. Yellow with a black centre.'

'Exactly. When you hit that centre, stop dead and make a big jump to the left. A really big one, straight left. Got that? Make sure you're clear of that spot because I shall be aiming my pounce at it. Then go hard round back into the room and straight under the china cabinet. Keep up your best speed all the way because I'll be coming after you and I don't want to look slow.'

'OK. I've got the picture.'

Hannibal looked over his shoulder again. 'We'd better get on with it,' he said hurriedly. 'I think they've noticed me looking in here.'

His head disappeared. Seconds later Scratchbelly felt the bucket rock and tilt under a violent impact. It tilted further and he could hear Hannibal's claws scrabbling towards the top as he leant his full weight against it. Slowly the bucket leaned over, then suddenly began to fall.

Scratchbelly leapt as it fell and came down running. Hannibal had aimed well. He had only to adjust his course slightly to put himself in line for the door. Resisting the urge to swerve away from the table, where the Humans' roars and movements showed that they were well aware of his presence, he went straight for the doorway, uncomfortably aware that Hannibal was rapidly closing the gap. Then he was on the mat: he made a short spring to its black centre, then leapt high and long to the left. Out of the corner of his eye he saw Hannibal's front claws strike the mat beside him: the sight spurred him to even greater speed. The friendly gloom beneath the china cabinet beckoned. He rushed gratefully into the shadow, dived towards the hole – and then, unthinking in his surprise, swerved away. For the hole was occupied – blocked – by a mouse. Nutcruncher, grinning unpleasantly and shaking his head meaningfully, was planted firmly in the entrance.

8

His surprise at this appalling, unheard-of breach of the Mouse Code robbed Scratchbelly of thought at a crucial moment. He swerved to the left, and found to his horror that his speed had taken him clear of the shelter of the cabinet and into the corner of the room. Meanwhile, Hannibal, sheering away left-handed after a well-simulated despairing lunge, came to a slithering halt in the same corner. His eyes widened as they focused on

Scratchbelly standing centimetres in front of his claws.

'This is bad,' he said solemnly. 'What happened?'

Scratchbelly told him.

'Nasty. Really not right,' said Hannibal. 'But – the fact is . . . I'm sorry Scratchbelly, but I've got to do it I'm afraid. I can't afford to let you off. The Humans are watching.'

'I know. I knew as soon as I swerved. Should have gone the other way, but – there it is. No hard feelings, Hannibal. But make it quick, please.'

'Sure,' said the cat sadly. 'Well, here goes.'

He drew himself back slightly, tensed his rear leg muscles – then spun round suddenly at a sudden commotion round the table. The Humans were roaring and pointing at a chair at the end of it. On its back the small figure of Sidestepper perched precariously, watching the Humans intently and poised for instant flight.

Hannibal turned swiftly and briefly back to

Scratchbelly. 'It would seem,' he said, grinning, 'that Sidestepper has got us both off the hook.' Then he swung away and raced across the floor, shouting at the top of his voice. 'Right, Sidestepper! Straight down the table and keep your ears open. We'll make it up as we go along!'

As in most unrehearsed performances, mistakes happened. Sidestepper leapt lightly on to the table and dashed down the tablecloth as instructed – but the Male Human grabbed a knife and fork and began stabbing vigorously at him. Sidestepper had to live up to his name, checking, swerving and skipping as fork and knife plunged alternately towards him.

'Right! Jump off to the right!' yelled Hannibal. It was unfortunate that at that moment Sidestepper was forced to perform a pirouette to avoid a particularly accurate jab from the fork and was facing back to where he had come from, with the result that, responding automatically to Hannibal's call, he leapt off the wrong side of the table.

Hannibal, expecting the mouse to fall on the far side, was surprised to find Sidestepper dropping through the air directly above him.

Hannibal was equal to the situation. In a flash he rolled on his back and swung a paw, the claws retracted. Sidestepper was batted through the air beneath the table and landed clear of it on his back, on the carpet. Hannibal had been somewhat too vigorous: the mouse was clearly visible and the Male Human, who was on that side of the table, gave a shout and raised a foot with the clear intention of stamping Sidestepper into the floor.

Sidestepper righted himself as the great shoe was poised to descend. He sprang forward, found himself confronted by the Human's standing leg and, in desperation, leapt upward, clutched the cloth of the trousers and hung on.

The Human's response was spectacular. He gave a startled bellow and kicked high with his mouse-bearing leg – neglecting in his haste to ensure that his other foot had first returned to earth – and ended flat on his back in consequence. He was, however, successful in removing Sidestepper, who was flung high in the air towards the Female Human. She ducked involuntarily and Sidestepper flew an inch above her upturned face, the mouth wide open in a high-pitched howl.

The rest of the chase was relatively straightforward. Sidestepper landed on the carpet, halfway to the hall door. Fortunately it was open and Hannibal, who had been watching the proceedings closely while pretending to carry out a confused search under the table, shouted to him to go for it. Sidestepper was dazed and winded but he obeyed as soon as he had worked out where he was. He ran wearily towards the doorway, accelerating as he heard Hannibal call, 'Get moving! I'm coming!'

Hannibal loped swiftly – but not too swiftly – across the room and went through the doorway close behind the mouse. The sitting-room door

on the other side of the hall was closed;
Hannibal glanced behind quickly to ensure that
the Humans were not following, leapt lightly
over Sidestepper and flung himself at it. The
door opened about six inches. 'Fireplace,'
said Hannibal brusquely. Sidestepper nodded
and passed through. 'Don't hang about;
they're coming,' said Hannibal urgently, darting
through himself and heading for the window,
the top of which was open as usual. He began
jumping and squalling energetically while
Sidestepper, now almost spent, tottered to the
fireplace and climbed thankfully up to the loose
brick and safety.

9

Scratchbelly had been anxiously watching the chase from his corner, tensing each time Sidestepper came close to disaster. Finally he relaxed as the mouse and the cat disappeared into the hall, satisfied that all would be well; then he turned abruptly and marched fiercely towards the hole under the china cabinet, ready for battle. The hole was, however, empty – and so was the run behind it.

As he entered the main chamber Scratchbelly

collided with Slickwhiskers, who was leaving it in some haste. She gave a squeal of relieved surprise.

'We thought you were dead,' she said bluntly.

'What happened?'

The departure of Scratchbelly and Sidestepper had, apparently, been noticed; and Nutcruncher had taken the opportunity to invade Scratchbelly territory, waiting until Tailtwist was out foraging before charging into the living chamber with four of the largest of his brood. Slickwhiskers and three of her young were in residence, together with Old Grey. They managed to hold the chamber entrance against their more powerful adversaries but were unable to drive them back, and had been in effect imprisoned in the chamber. Nutcruncher had taken great delight in describing Hannibal's pursuit of Scratchbelly, shouting it from the hole entrance and ending with: 'He thinks he's safe but he's not getting in here – he's catfood.' Then there was silence;

and Slickwhiskers had only just realized that the Nutcrunchers had left the run when Scratchbelly appeared.

Scratchbelly in turn told Slickwhiskers all that had happened to him and Sidestepper. Slickwhiskers was worrying about Sidestepper and Scratchbelly was reassuring her when they were interrupted by the arrival of Flickerear.

'Excuse me, sir,' she said loudly, 'but there's a deputation to see you.'

The politeness of the tone and form of her speech – so much in contrast with her normal off-handedness – made Scratchbelly look up in surprise. Standing behind Flickerear he recognized Nutcruncher's mate Brindle and one of her offspring, a light-coloured mouse big for his age.

'Good day, Brindle – Number Six,' he said coolly. And then, not to be outdone by his offspring in politeness, 'Thank you Flickerear. You may go.'

'Yes sir,' said Flickerear demurely, and

withdrew, rolling her eyes at him as she went out to confirm what he already knew, that this was a performance wholly for the Nutcrunchers' benefit.

'Now, Brindle, you have something to say?' He approved of Brindle, knowing her to have intelligence far beyond that of her mate. She was bright-eyed and sharp-nosed, somewhat haggard from the demands of her numerous young but full of spirit. She faced him resolutely.

'Scratchbelly, I'm here to apologize for my mate's behaviour. Blocking the hole to you – it was totally unethical, quite unforgivable. We all know that assistance must be given against Predators, whatever differences there may be between us.'

Scratchbelly nodded and held his peace, wondering where his request to Hannibal concerning the kitchen area came in the ethical scheme.

'I have decided,' continued Brindle, 'that I

cannot remain with a clan leader who resorts to such behaviour. I am leaving as soon as possible and taking my four youngest – my last litter – with me. Number Six agrees with me and is coming too.'

'Where will you go?' said Scratchbelly anxiously. He was genuinely concerned for their future. 'The Open is a dangerous place.'

Number Six answered. 'We shall go to the Shed. It's cold, and we shall have to dig runs under the floor, but the compost heap is close by. We shall have cover and plenty to eat.'

'Yes, but Seizer is kept in there now, isn't he? For some of the time, anyway. Or so I believe,' he ended hurriedly, not wanting to point up his association with Hannibal.

'That's right, sir,' said Number Six. 'Personally, I think that's good. Seizer will shout about us but the Humans won't notice what he's on about. They'll tell him to shut up, probably. And he's no great shakes at actually catching mice. I reckon we'll be left in peace.'

Scratchbelly looked at him. 'Good. Very good,' he said. 'You are your mother's son, Number Six: you have brains.' He turned to Brindle. 'You said you were leaving as soon as possible. Does that mean immediately?'

'It does. My four youngest are waiting near the outside hole. I sent them there straightaway, to avoid meeting Nutcruncher.'

'Very well, Flickerear and I' – she had just re-entered the chamber – 'shall escort you to them.'

'Ahem,' said Number Six. It was a curious expression for a mouse. Scratchbelly looked at him in surprise. Then Flickerear spoke.

'I'm going with them, Dad.'

'Oh. Ah. Well . . . um.' Scratchbelly was still trying to make sense of this when Slickwhiskers came alongside him.

'I think that's an excellent idea,' she said decidedly. 'Number Six is an excellent choice, don't you think? Clearly a bright, well-built young mouse.' Then, in a harder but not

unkindly tone, to Flickerear: 'The garlic expedition, I suppose?'

Flickerear nodded.

The departure of Brindle, Flickerear and the others went off smoothly. On returning to the chamber Scratchbelly relaxed, and immediately remembered how hungry he was. He at once grabbed some sweetcorn intended for Old Grey (who protested furiously but to no avail) and was munching avidly when Slickwhiskers suddenly said, 'Shouldn't Sidestepper be here by now?'

'You're right.' Scratchbelly stopped in mid-munch. 'I'll go and find him.'

He went hurriedly down the run, anxiety mounting at every step. He had assumed that all was well, but perhaps the blow from Hannibal's paw or the flight through the air had been too much; it was not unknown for a mouse to continue his run to his hole only to expire in safety from shock or injury. He hurried to the fireplace, calling for Sidestepper as he went.

Sidestepper was lying comfortably by the broken brick.

'You took your time,' he said aggrievedly. 'After all the trouble I went to to save your skin, I was expecting a bit more parental concern.'

'That's right.' Hannibal's voice came from below. 'Thoughtless, I call it. Very uncaring.

Anybody'd think you were a male cat.'

'There have been developments,' said Scratchbelly apologetically, and told them of Brindle's visit. Sidestepper gave a whoop of delight.

'That evens things up pretty well,' he said. 'I'm sorry to lose Flickerear. But I think our numbers will soon be going up. I know for a fact that Tailtwist has found a mate in the garden. You've probably noticed he's been spending a lot of time in the Open.'

'As it happens, I had; but you might have told me why. Still' – Scratchbelly sighed – 'no doubt Slickwhiskers knows already. I trust he's bringing her into the house? Not going off somewhere else?'

'Oh no. He's staying put. She's a good, strong mouse, Dad. We need new blood.'

'Then I shall not object,' said Scratchbelly, uncomfortably aware that he was sounding very pompous and Old Greyish.

'This is all very well,' said Hannibal, 'but if

you lot are going to infest the place it seems to me I'm going to have to stay in business. Now and again, at any rate.'

The two mice looked at each other.

'I think,' said Scratchbelly slowly, 'we had better get over to the spice cupboard. We need to stock up on garlic.'